*

LITTLE BABY LYDIA

(Grandpa, Grandma, and student-mom: family role-reversal and the new times)

Oliver Akamnonu

Little Baby Lydia

Library of Congress Control Number: Pending

ISBN
> Hardcover 978-1-940909-17-2
> Softcover 978-1-940909-18-9
> e-book   978-1-940909-19-6

Printed in the USA

For additional copies of this book or for enquiries about the same
Contact the author, email: ooakams@yahoo.com
or contact
Akamnonu Associates Incorporated
www.akamnonuassociatesinc.com
Tel. (+1) 413-693-8428

Prologue

We who served our turns "long after they are gone"
We who devoted a good chunk of our younger lives
caring for offspring that were our own
And went the extra mile baby-sitting our
grandchildren so their parents could work or school;
We who relearnt to change babies' diapers,
even as we approached the stages of changing our
own with unsteady fingers
And learnt again to distinguish between cries of
wetness and cries of hunger in little babies;
And, again rocked fragile little infants to sleep even as
our own weary eyes craved for some sleep;
We who re-learnt the rhythms of old
and combined these with trending rhythms of the
moment;
And re-learnt the art of bottle-feeding fragile little
infants while their parents went to school;
We who passed sleepless nights soothing a grandchild
to sleep
And as grandmas and grandpas assumed the roles of
volunteer baby-sitters;
And observed with tender loving care every turn of
our little bundles of joy;
And observed the once tiny suckling babies mature to
giggling little angels;
To us, grandfathers and grandmothers, who, in times
of great need, faced up to the challenges
And nurtured with love and dedication, our infant
grandsons and granddaughters,
To us, and people who may not have the opportunity
to nurture, and yet, appreciate what we did

To us all, grandpas and grandmas, to you all young moms and young dads,
To well-wishing friends and loved ones far and near who read this story;
And very importantly to you Baby Lydia,
To you who have brought immeasurable joy to parents, family, kit and kin alike,
To you who have brought more joy daily than words alone could tell.
To you and all babies like you; and very sincerely to you, adorable Baby Lydia, this little book is dedicated.

Oliver Akamnonu

To Brandon, Bryan, Arinze and Somkene;
For bringing joy and fulfilment to every day of our lives.
And most importantly,
To you, Chikadibia:
If only all wives, all mothers and all grandmothers were like you.

Contents

Chapter 1

BETWEEN THE EXPECTANT MOTHER AND HER STUDIES

"I know it is an uphill task. But I am determined to make it", Nena reassured herself again as she stepped out of her car. She was obviously running late for the very important group discussion on "Diabetes Mellitus and childhood obesity" scheduled with a supervisor for that morning.

"It's tough, but I am determined to positively surprise my friends, my professors and any sceptics." Nena paused for a while to ensure that nobody was within hearing distance before continuing.

"I intend to prove that it is possible to still make the honors while combining schooling with being an expectant mother".

Nena was soliloquizing as if to reassure herself in the face of what appeared an increasingly difficult task before her. The physical and emotional stress that she was undergoing combining the challenges of medical school education with being a first-time expectant mother, was inexorably telling on her. She was thirty-four weeks pregnant and had just entered the final year of her medical school career.
During her ante-natal visit to her obstetrician earlier that day, Nena had been informed that her unborn baby was not gaining weight as ascertained by physical measurements and by ultrasound results.

"You may have to be delivered by induction a little before the due date if after a further two weeks we do not see good progress in the fetal weight" Nena's doctor, Dr. Paul had informed her.

Nena was making all efforts not to allow her pregnancy and impending childbirth to prevent her from graduating with her classmates in the final year medicine class of her medical school in Boston Massachusetts. She was thirty years old and had for some years been considering having a baby before turning thirty-one since she was so fond of babies. She would definitely wish to have her own baby before completing her medical school education. She was however a bit apprehensive about how she would be able to combine nursing a new-born baby with her very rigorous academic pursuits.

Nena had just completed her posting in pediatrics and neonatology earlier that year. While her fiancé Dave was visiting from Johannesburg South Africa, Nena and the latter had decided that she would not wait till she graduated from the medical school before starting a family. This was contrary to the opinion of many of Nena's married or seriously engaged female classmates who Nena often discussed with.
"From all indications, the remotest possibility of Down's syndrome or some age-related abnormality or diminished fertility, is not what any medically-enlightened mother would want to toy with if it could be avoided", Nena had further earlier muted to herself.

"Even with any, and all equivocations, I would not wish to be an elderly primigravida. No, not with all the associated risks. I would not wish to swim in quick-sand or to fly at the face of providence, the astonishing strides in medical and reproductive science notwithstanding." Nena further said to herself. "If I had not spent some time doing a Masters Degree program I would have preferred to be fully done with the medical school before starting my family." Nena said.

She had spent countless hours considering her many options. On each occasion she had always arrived at the same conclusion as shared by majority of her female classmates that it was better to wait awhile and complete her medical school before starting a family.

"But then I would not want to toy with problems associated with unduly delayed pregnancy and childbirth even with the much progress made in the field of obstetrics and gynecology."

Nena had reasoned with Dave as the two recently-engaged young people discussed during Dave's brief vacation from his overseas job location earlier-on in the year.

Nena's mom, Agesi, lived with her husband Oguebe in the small city of Sunderland some one hundred and sixteen miles further West of Boston.

Agesi had often been quietly concerned about possible decreasing chances of her only daughter's biological motherhood since the latter often appeared averse to discussions about the subject with her. Not only was Nena the only daughter, she was the only child from the thirty-two-year-old marriage between Agesi and her husband Oguebe.

"My own mother was a college-educated school teacher and had fertility problems associated with delayed marriage and pregnancy. She was too engrossed with her academic pursuit in those early days of western education in our homeland. She ended up getting married in her mid-thirties. She had her first baby after eight years of marriage. That baby was me, and my mother's pregnancy was possible only after medical intervention. She had to try for a further eight years of marriage before she had her second baby in what was described at that time as a near obstetric-miracle." Agesi said.

"Obviously my mother would have wanted more babies since that was in a clime where the average family had five or more children. But my mother begot my little sister and me only after series of medical interventions. I understood that her fertility problems stemmed largely from her postponement of marriage and motherhood for educational reasons. I would therefore want to have my daughter marry not later than age thirty. She should start her family early." Agesi further lamented.

Agesi had often narrated her stories in the presence of Nena. It was as if she was persuading Nena not to make the same "mistake" which her grandmother made. Agesi herself would have wanted more children but apparently that did not materialize.
Being the only child, Nena was particularly close to her mother. And she readily shared mom's views about the need to start her family without further delay. She had followed up her decision by encouraging her fiancée who lived a world away in Johannesburg South Africa, to visit regularly, the high cost of air travel notwithstanding.

By the time Nena got into the lecture room there were only a handful of the students already assembled. Many of the students lived in shared apartments around the school. They therefore often set out for the lecture rooms shortly before scheduled lecture times believing they would never be late. Thus, it was, that most of the students who lived very close to the school often either came late or came into classes almost at the last minute before lectures. That was unlike Nena and a few others who lived a little further away and who consequently often set out earlier to beat the heavy Boston traffic.

Just as Nena brought out her iPad to check for any mails before the onset of the discussions, her good friend Tiffany who also lived quite some distance away from the school also entered and sat close to Nena.
"Hi, Nena! So, so ironical that we who live furthest away from the school are often the earliest to arrive for class events."
"Yes, that is the way it often is. That's why it is often said that they who live closest the church are often the late comers to Sunday worship."
"And how are you coping with the upcoming baby, Nena?" Tiffany asked.
"It's obviously challenging but at the same time exciting. I always look forward to seeing the real looks of the new baby. But I find that I sometimes feel too tired these days after the day's work, quite unlike before the pregnancy." Nena replied.
"That is perhaps why they called it 'expectant mother'. You will always be expecting to have a real-life look of the new baby." Tiffany empathized.

Tiffany was one of Nena's best friends in the class. She was of native American ancestry and she was very fond of discussing intimately with Nena who she often addressed as "My sister Nee-Nee".

Further discussion about the challenges of pregnancy for an active student between the two friends was cut short by the entry into the classroom of the day's discussion moderator.

Chapter 2.

DAD AND MOM, A SECOND MISSIONARY JOURNEY

Nena had concluded her arrangements with her doctor for her induction scheduled for the last Saturday of September. Repeat ultrasound had shown that the baby was still not gaining the expected weight even after a further two weeks of observation. A determination had therefore been made that it was safer to deliver the baby by induction especially since it was already entering into the 38th week of pregnancy.

"Your baby is safer out now than in", Nena's doctor had told her. And so was it.
Dad and mom had been preparing for a further two or three weeks before they would become grandparents. They had started preparing for their new roles as grandparents with the attendant joys and responsibilities since Nena was at a crucial stage of her educational pursuits.

Rigorous search for a live-in nanny had so far yielded no fruits. The very good Day-care centers in town were fully-booked. The not-so-good but registered ones were also not immediately available.
Applicants in need of Day-care services had queued up waiting for spaces. Most had registered well in advance of
the times that they wished to bring in their children or wards.

In Nena's inexperience she had not thought of Day-care services until she was almost due for delivery. Agesi and Oguebe had completed child-rearing well before they immigrated to the United States. They were therefore not conversant with the many child-care problems existent in the American society. They therefore had not advised their daughter and her fiancé about the need to book early for good Day-care services.

Even the little-known and relatively unpopular Day-care centers were not there for the asking. Even in those so-called "economy-class Day-care centers", there was invariably a waiting period of some weeks or "until a vacancy is available".

It was therefore only the private and unregistered, often private home-based, individually-run centers that had spaces for people who did not register in advance. Many of the latter had no sign-boards and did not advertise on-line. They were therefore mostly discovered by recommendation or by wide searches through friends and church members.

Events were to be rapidly fast-forwarded.

Again, Dave, Nena' fiancé and the father of the expected baby, lived in Johannesburg in far-away South Africa. He was expected to come in even if briefly by the 39th week. He had applied for, and had only two weeks earlier succeeded in securing temporary work permit in the United States pending the materialization of full immigrant status to join his prospective new family.

Dave and Nena had for too long been postponing legalization and formalization of their union. They had planned to have a hurried wedding prior to the delivery of the baby as soon as Dave arrived to the United States. But events turned out otherwise.

"I had always wanted to have a great wedding ceremony prior to my having my first baby. But I guess I will have to change my plans in the light of the changed situations", Nena said.
Obviously with the earlier-than-planned arrival of the baby arrangements had to change very quickly too.

"We may now have to wait forever, or at least until the baby would be old enough to be our flower-girl!". Nena had jokingly told Dave during their telephone conversation just after the verdict of Nena's obstetrician regarding the need for early induction.
"It's no problem, Nena. Many of my friends did not even bother about church weddings. None of these religious ceremonies ever guarantees success of any union". Dave said.
"No, they may not guarantee success or stability or a happy married life, Dave, but almost every woman loves to have a great wedding album." Nena said.
"I know, but no wedding album states that a wedding was a first or a fifth, or whether it was celebrated before or after the couple had had all their children or not. My own parents wedded only after they had my six siblings and me. Indeed, my two elder sisters and my two younger sisters were the flower girls and my twin brother and I, were the page boys during my mother's wedding to my father!
I always imagined what fun it would be to have a similar scenario between us, a scenario where our sons and daughters would be our flower girls and page boys." Dave said laughing out loud over the phone.

"Ha, ha, ha, Dave, it looks like you persuaded the American Consulate in Pretoria to purposely delay the processing of your U.S work papers so you could spend more time in South Africa. Looks like you love Johannesburg life very much", Nena said.
"No, Nena. "Dave said. "I certainly will be in Boston at the earliest possible moment. I certainly would not wish to be told the stories. I will like to be physically there to witness the arrival of my daughter."

As soon as the conversation with Dave was over, Nena dialed her parents. She could not reach either of them. She therefore left messages for them:
"Dad and mom, you guys just have to come down quickly. I have also informed Dave of the changed arrangements. I expect he will fly in to Boston's Logan Airport before the induction of labor starts in forty-eight hours' time. Surely Dave cannot afford to miss the moment of arrival of his daughter. At least so he says. And unless he misses his flight or the flight gets canceled I expect he will be here any time soon. We have been planning for this for quite some time, but the previously-unplanned induction two weeks earlier, was not factored into the equation" Nena said.

Agesi called her husband soon after she listened to Nena's message.
"O.G, did you get Nena's message? Looks like our granddaughter will arrive sooner than we had planned." Agesi told Oguebe as soon as the latter picked up the phone.
"Yes, A.G, I have just listened to the message too. It certainly is going to be rough with both parents living so widely apart. It is certainly not easy to be a single parent, no matter how temporarily."

"Well, it may mean that we, the baby's grandparents, living a hundred miles away may have to shoulder the greater burden after Nena's delivery until Dave finally relocates fully to the U.S."
"But even when Dave relocates, with Nena being in school, how do they begin to care for a newborn baby without experience and with the attendant difficulties of procuring a babysitter and house help in general, in Boston? And none of us is fully retired so as to put in full time for them at least until they can sort themselves out!", Oguebe said.

"O.G, a solution has to be found once the baby arrives. It may be a difficult solution but there has to be a short-term solution nonetheless." Agesi said in her characteristic forthright manner.
"You are right A.G, we have to plan well and perhaps think twice as fast. The new baby obviously cannot wait. She will need full attention from day one." Oguebe said.

It was not break period and since Agesi worked in a busy clinic, she did not have the luxury of long telephone discussions during office hours. Indeed, she had made the call only because it was a very important message from Nena.
Although Oguebe was privately employed he too did not have the luxury of long telephone conversations during office hours.
"Two weeks have elapsed almost as rapidly as two days." Agesi said.
"Yes, Agesi, I think it was Henry Van Dyke who stated that time is too slow for those who wait, and too swift for those who fear." Oguebe said.
"You and those your big grammar poets, O.G. Good a thing you are about to have grandchildren who you can impart your many quotations to."

"Yes, Agesi, Van Dyke also stated that when it concerns planning to become a grandparent it is equivalent to passage of time for those who love. In this latter situation time, again according to Van Dyke, becomes 'an eternity'." Oguebe who was a great fan of literary classics quoted to a rather non-literary-inclined Agesi when the couple got home from work that evening.

"Well, I don't know about eternity, O.G. All I know is that it is not going to be easy for Nena and Dave as regards care for their arriving baby daughter. Perhaps there should have been better planning well ahead of time." Agesi said, again, in her usually very blunt and realistic manner.

"Let the grandchildren come on, Agesi! Let them come on in droves. We are here! The worst that can happen is that we take all of them with us to Sunderland. We have enough space in our home. After all, our parents used to have upwards of six to ten children and they took care of them adequately. And this is just our first granddaughter. Supposing we had five of them as our own children, won't we take care of them. And five children are only half of the number of children that my own mother had. And she took care of us all and adequately too."

"Did you say adequately, O.G?" Agesi asked.

"Yes, adequately! Do I look like one whose mother did not take care of adequately? Do I look malnourished? Or do I look mentally or physically retarded from malnutrition? And they said that my grandmother had nine children! And did you ever hear that any of my siblings or any of Nena's uncles or aunties was malnourished or was not well brought up?" Oguebe asked, feigning some seriousness.

"O.G, you are talking of the early and mid-twentieth century. And you are also referring to events in the developing world. We are in the twenty-first century, and in the developed world. When we compare, it should be apples with apples, and not apples with oranges.

"Remember, this is the United States of America. And we are way into the twenty-first century. Again, remember we are talking of Boston Massachusetts metropolis!" Agesi emphasized.

"Very well, very well, Agesi, whatever you say, but let the grandchildren come!" Oguebe concluded. He knew he would not win the argument. And he wanted to put a quick end to it.

It was a Friday. The induction of labor was scheduled for the next day, Saturday. Nena was expected to check in at the maternity section of the Boston Hospital by 6pm.

As soon as Oguebe and Agesi got home from work they quickly gathered a few personal effects and were on their way to Boston.

It was mid-September and the golden-yellow evening sun of late summer was still joyously piercing through the characteristically-boisterous New England evening clouds at that time of year. But neither Agesi nor Oguebe appeared to notice or relish the beautiful and artistic designs made by the many jet planes that crisscrossed the horizon, some heading to Bradley International Airport, some to Logan International Airport, and many others to the numerous smaller local airports that dotted the landscape in Western Massachusetts.

Not even the melodious music that emanated from the FM radio of the car appeared to attract the attention of either traveler.

It was supposed to be a thing of joy expecting the arrival of one's first granddaughter. But the fear of the unknown in pregnancy and childbirth appeared to dull the enthusiasm even in that most sophisticated of circumstances.

On their previous drives to Boston Agesi and Oguebe would usually sing along most of the music verses of the familiar tunes as emanated from their car CD. But that particular evening was different. On that day Nena, their daughter, was expected to check into the maternity section of Boston University Hospital for the induction to have her baby.

Some fifteen miles into the journey Nena had again called.

"How far away are you mom and dad? I have already finished packing my stuff awaiting your arrival. But drive carefully. Don't rush, I am fine".

Nena did not sound frantic or distressed, not even anxious.

"Nena, you must be very courageous, you have already completed packing your things for the hospital admission. I thought that you would be panicking and so might not be ready", Agesi told her daughter.

"No, mom, I am really excited. I can't wait to see the real-life face of my baby. I know labor is gonna be painful but I will bear it. I will resist epidural injection. I guess the joy of delivery will be more if one goes through the pains the old-fashioned way. One of my classmates and friend, Tessy, who had epidural during her delivery said that she did not feel any pains when the baby popped out and that she did not quite like it. She said that she had earlier requested for epidural when the labor pains became unbearable, but that she later wished that she had endured the pains to serve as a constant reminder of the birth of her baby." Nena said gleefully.

"We wait till we get there Nena. We will pray to God that everything goes on without any hitches." Agesi said.

"Mortality and morbidity associated with childbirth in the United States are very negligible mom. But we will still pray that all goes well."

"Shall we still stop at the Natick Service Station to stretch our legs as usual, or do we give the snacks and soda a miss today?" Oguebe asked Agesi as soon as the latter concluded her rather lengthy phone conversation with Nena.

"No, Agesi, today is a little different. We will give the roadside snacks a miss today and head straight to Boston. Nena must be counting the seconds"

The heavy traffic that usually characterized the approach to the Cambridge Massachusetts exit near Boston was unusually light that evening. The smoothness of the traffic prompted Oguebe who had been unusually reticent throughout the journey to say: "Thank God, it looks like God knows how pressed I am to use the bathroom not having stopped at any of the service stations. The traffic is unusually light today."

Agesi and Oguebe were soon at Nena's Dorchester Harbor Point apartment.

As she and Oguebe entered Nena's apartment they saw three bags already packaged and standing in the corridor adjacent to the living room.

Agesi had expected to see her daughter nervous or at least anxious-looking. But she was surprised to see a vibrant and hilarious Nena in a bear hug with her, even in spite of her late pregnant abdomen.

"You don't seem to be anxious honey. I am happy you are quite strong and active for this stage of pregnancy."

"Yes, of course I am a little nervous mom. Who wouldn't be? But at the same time, I am excited at the expectation of my new baby. She keeps kicking me in the upper abdomen and sometimes I feel that I can feel her heels." Nena said.

During the twelve-minute drive to the hospital Oguebe tried to lighten the moment by narrating stories about how excited he and his medical student classmates used to be as they struggled to secure the deliveries needed for completion of their obstetric postings. But in spite of the funny stories, intermittent periods of silence confirmed the inherent anxiety on the faces of the occupants of the car. The lightest moment of the short drive was when a call came from Dave, Nena's fiancé that he would arrive Logan Airport within an hour. On being told that the family was already on their way to the hospital he said that he would head straight to the hospital from the airport.

"Ensure you don't pop out the baby before my arrival Nena. I will like to cut the umbilical cord by myself" Dave joked over the phone.

"Hurry up Dave, so you share in the pains of labor. I will inform the baby to stay put in the womb until you arrive to the delivery room." Nena replied with equal hilarity.

"We will have to ensure that they don't start your induction until Dave clears through the secure area of the airport. You can sometimes never fully predict how soon full contractions start when once the induction is started. And you cannot turn back the hand of the clock once established labor starts." Oguebe said.

For Nena it was a novelty, the dawn of a new era. But for Agesi who had her baby more than a quarter century earlier, it was like a second missionary journey.

Chapter 3

LEARNING TO KEEP UP WITH A NEW LIFE

The maternity section of the Boston Hospital was meticulously and impeccably constructed. Neither Oguebe nor Agesi had had cause to visit a maternity section of any hospital in the United States. A lot of things were automated. And the large traffic of pregnant women, some of them in early stages of labor, did not appear to stress the attending staff who all appeared very professional in their attitude to visitors and patients.
Because of the heavy traffic on the road from Dorchester to the Medical Center and the large number of vehicles queueing up at the drop-off point in front of the hospital, it took quite some time to finally get to the last entry point into the maternity section proper. However, the party had set out quite early and had arrived well ahead of the scheduled time for induction.

Just before Nena and the duo of Agesi and Oguebe walked up to the last security-coded door leading into the proper maternity section, a tall young man clutching a small traveling bag and a cup of ice tea was seen rushing towards the expectant mother and her parents. It was Dave. He had barely made it from the airport before the party would get into the assigned induction room. It was a near-miracle that he made it just in time before the party crossed the final security checkpoint. It would have been difficult for him to be let in separately if he arrived a mere one-minute latter.

The induction was a scheduled procedure and all arrangements had been completed to receive the expectant mother.

Within a short time of being called up at the reception an identification arm band and a loose "nativity gown" were adorning the wrist of the new "customer". The three family members who accompanied Nena were also given identification arm bands and were allowed in with her. It was a far cry from what usually obtained in the maternity section of Agesi's former hospital where there was restriction of family members except the spouse where applicable, from labor to after delivery. Perhaps there was in the prevailing circumstances, a greater realization of the crucial role of family in encouraging and uplifting the would-be mother at such moments of great need, the pains of child birth.

The series of wide corridors with security-fitted automatic doors, finally led to the correct induction room that had been prepared for Nena. There was no more room for anxiety as events began to move like clockwork.

The preliminary routine physical checks and routine preparations were conducted and the infusion line was set up with the initial drug infusions.

Nena appeared very relaxed especially with the presence of Dave and with her parents beside her.

Agesi was very supportive lightning the moment with stories of her experiences on the day that she had Nena.

"I had gone to work as usual and had come back with no signs of impending labor." She told Nena.

"It was just before dinner that I felt slight tingling sensations in my lower abdomen. It was twelve days before the expected date of labor and I was counting on possibility of onset of labor in a further one week.

It was only when I visited the bathroom that I realized that I was indeed in my first stage s of labor. Since Agesi was not around, just like Dave was almost not around, I had called on my neighbor who happened to be a nurse and she accompanied me to the maternity. I drove the car and indeed had stopped by two different stores to purchase materials needed by the maternity. It was not like the maternity sections here where you came in with virtually nothing and almost everything would be provided by the hospital. In our original part of the world, you had to check in with almost everything that you would need during labor and delivery."

Agesi's short narration obviously fascinated Nena and must have lightened her mood. Her earlier stoic demeanor was beginning to melt after the donning of maternity gown and the sight of so many nurses and gadgets. The delivery room soon appeared to be swarming with nurses, Obstetrics Residents and one or two others who appeared to be medical students. Yet it was all so very orderly.
It was almost solemn, even for Nena who had clerked and participated in a number of cases during her obstetric posting.

"Even though I have seen and used some of these gadgets, I feel a little nervous mom. It's a different thing when one is the patient." Nena said.
"Yes, I know. The realities dawn on the individual when he or she is the subject of a procedure." Agesi replied, in obvious empathy with her daughter.
For the first one hour or so after the commencement of induction the drops from the drip-stand did not appear to be of much significance. But soon the inevitable onset of contractions began to set in.

Nena who at first smiled and gently stroked her abdomen could now be seen slightly twisting her face at the onset of the contractions which as expected began to appear at shorter intervals and gradually-increasing intensity.

The gentle twisting of the face soon progressed to tight squeezing of Dave's and Agesi's palms on either side of the bed. The squeezing increased in tightness at the onset of each subsequent wave of contractions. Then came the screams which grew louder and more intense.

The young lady who had promised herself that she would "not scream at my arriving baby girl" was soon to throw overboard all promises and all bravado. Like her friend and classmate Tessy, she had further earlier vowed that she would refuse administration of epidural to control her pains. The intensifying pains readily made her change her mind.

"I can no longer bear it mom!", she screamed continuously.

"Nurse, please this pain must be stopped! Anything that will stop the pains!"

Oguebe looked on helplessly. He wished he could do something to help her daughter, even when he knew that the pains were very temporary.

The pains of labor are no friend of even the strongest. They can compel even the strongest to disavow any promises.

"With anguish and great pains, you shall bring forth children" so stated the Holy Book in Genesis.

If the book of Genesis must be believed, Eve must have done great disservice to humanity by attracting the punishment.

But is it really a punishment?

No, it is a labor of love. For, out of such pains a new human being, loving and tender, is brought into the world! Oguebe muted to himself.

He had hitherto maintained unusual silence since the party's arrival at the maternity ward. He would obviously have preferred to receive the news of the delivery at home especially since Dave and Agesi were already around. But he and Agesi felt that they owed it as a duty to their daughter to be with her at that moment of great need.

When it became obvious that the pains were overbearing for Nena, the anesthesiologist was called in. She got her materials together and administered epidural. It was professionally done and almost painlessly too.

The contractions thereafter continued but without the screams. It was a very welcome situation.

The arrival of the baby was the climax of the day's event. The umbilical cord was around the neck. But the delivery was professionally managed. It was a safe delivery of a "bouncing healthy baby girl".

Little Baby Lydia came into the world apparently like no other! She came in starry-eyed, opening her eyes and gazing around within five minutes of delivery! She appeared to want to miss nothing. And so, she stared around the delivery room without blinking an eyelid. She was such a strong baby. Her first cry was strong but brief. And her two clenched fists were in no time thrust into her mouth. It was a moment that grandpa and grandma would never forget.

Nena and Dave were filled with joy. Dave had been handed the scissors and he cut the umbilical cord of her daughter. It was probably a task that Dave had not expected hence his apparent surprise on being asked by the nurses to perform that duty. He was later to acknowledge that it was the greatest honor that was done to him.

Oguebe and Agesi, too were surprised since it was not the practice in their original part of the world. Nena smiled broadly at the first cry of her baby and her gaze never deviated from the mounted baby's cot as Baby Lydia was being tidied up. The traditional handing of the baby to the parents, Nena and Dave as well as the first introduction to breast milk were the crowning of Nena's joys.
Baby Lydia's first bonding with the mother at breast feeding was not missed by Oguebe's cameras which did not miss any stage of the delivery process at Nena's earlier request.
By the following morning, Grandma and Grandpa also had the opportunity of carrying their granddaughter. It was particularly joyful to Grandpa who, while his own daughter grew up did not quite have all the necessary time with her because of the pressures of work in his very busy practice.

Nena was luckier. At Baby Lydia's delivery both the latter's parents and grandparents were with her and had indeed posed for a group photograph with her shortly after her birth.

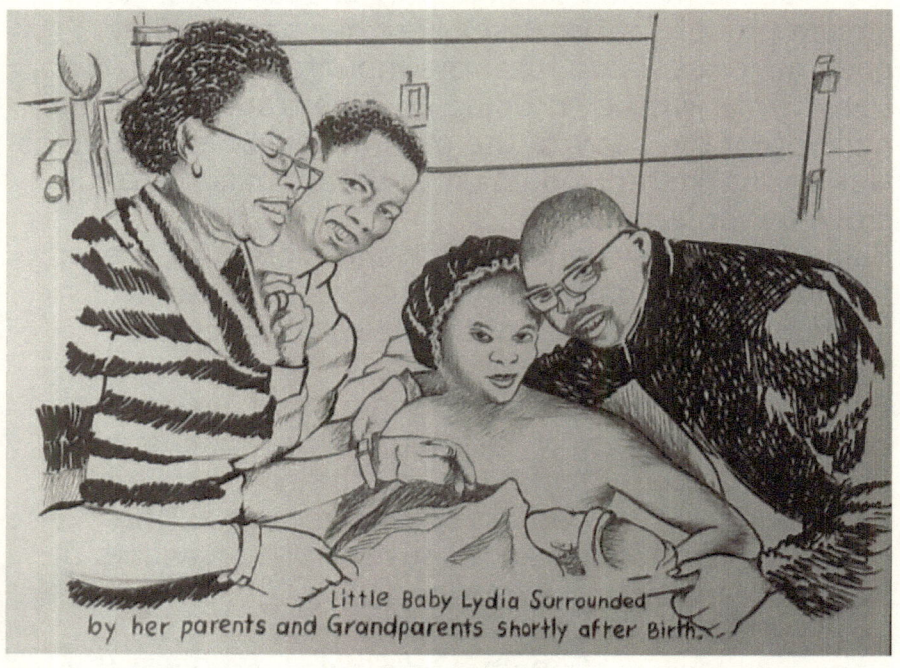

Little Baby Lydia Surrounded by her parents and Grandparents shortly after Birth.

Chapter 4

THE LITTLE LADY THAT MADE THE RULES

Agesi and Oguebe had all but forgotten how it looked like to nurse newborn babies. It had been nearly three decades since they had their last baby. Even though they were both in the medical profession, it was a different thing directing from a distance than being in the actual arena.

The baby appeared to them to be unusually tiny and fragile. She weighed almost six pounds at birth but she appeared so very tiny to handle. Both grandparents had all but lost touch about the size and fragility of the newborn. Oguebe in particular appeared unsure of where to handle the fragile little infant from. In the past, he had often voiced his admiration of pediatricians and had always marveled at how they were able to cope handling tiny little new-born babies.

"I always felt that the new-born babies were so fragile that their bones might break if slightly mishandled." Oguebe usually said.

But with the arrival of Little Baby Lydia, he had no option but to learn.

Agesi speedily adapted and once again became very proficient with handling the newborn just as if she had practiced the art repeatedly over the recent days.

Oguebe carried the fragile little *object* that was neatly wrapped to the neck in swaddling clothes, with utmost care. He carried the newborn baby who was covered head to toe save for the exposed face, almost as he would handle some breakable eggs.
Yes, little Baby Lydia was strong, yet so fragile-looking.
Yes, she appeared almost as fragile as some freshly-laid birds' eggs.

As he carried the little newborn on his palms, Oguebe hummed a new verse:
"The fragile nature of the newborn is a mystery to behold.
Its tumultuous debut into the world is even a greater mystery to witness
'Puny, but resilient', only partially describes the strength of the newborn.
The muscular adult man that touts his strength would do well to ponder awhile.
The strength of the tiny, little newborn far surpasses all imagination, man for man.
The cry is shrill and the palms fan out in Morro reflex, but these may only deceive.
The true evidence of its strength lies in the ability of the infant to withstand the rigors of its birth."

Nothing could be truer than Oguebe's hurriedly-composed verse.
Certainly, the ability of the new-born to withstand the rigors of delivery far surpass what the ordinary imagination of man can figure. It remains a mystery which is almost always taken for granted.

Different teams of nurses worked on the mother and the baby.
Both needed attention but to varying degrees.

Little Baby Lydia was soon comfortable and was wrapped in her tiny striped little "swaddling clothes". Nena needed much more attention, though beaming with smiles.

Even with her own needs in the immediate post-delivery period, mother's gaze never deviated from her new-born baby.
The entire procedure was so professionally done that Oguebe could not help commending the medical and nursing teams profusely, and openly.
"We thank God for his protection, and we thank you all for your care." He repeatedly said.

A grandpa that was not regular with his prayers could no longer conceal his appreciation and gratitude to God.
The safe and successful entrance of a first granddaughter into the world deserved more encomiums, appreciation and thanksgiving than mere words could give.
Though not always a bed of roses, life is weightier than all silver and gold.
And most of the blessings that we take for granted are not universally bestowed.
Religiosity or unflinching non-belief, are here out of the question.
The mystery in the advent of a new child is beyond any, and all arguments.
Rationalizations about Special Creation, even if scientifically unproven, or of Darwinism, no matter how well articulated, as in the latter case, are discussions for another day.

At day break, Oguebe needed to get back to the house while Agesi and Dave stayed behind with Nena and the newborn Little Baby Lydia.

Mother and her newborn baby were soon transferred to a room in the post-natal section of the maternity wing. It was well after Nena was settled into her room that Oguebe felt relaxed enough to take a closer look around the room and the facilities therein.

The post-natal room was like a five-star hotel room with full compliments of necessary hospital facilities for mother and newborn baby. Oguebe was very impressed by what he witnessed both in terms of equipment and care. It was all so fascinating, a completely different world from all accounts for Oguebe in comparison with the delivery rooms of his medical school years in the developing world.

By all accounts relating to allowing peace of mind to her parents and family, Baby Lydia was a very good baby. She rarely cried even when wet. She slept most of the time, waking up intermittently to feed. Early breastfeeding which the hospital strongly recommended was strictly adhered to by Nena.

In addition to the excellent and very professional job done earlier by the delivery-room medical staff, the Attending Obstetrician as well as the full team of pediatricians had come on the day following delivery and had thoroughly examined Nena and the new-born respectively. By the third day baby and mother were found fit enough for discharge. That was after pediatrician examination and attention as were found necessary.

It was a very fascinating experience for Oguebe and his household. The truth was that they came in as a family team of four and were leaving as a family team of five. Baby Lydia, the little new addition to the family team numbers, was sleeping peacefully in the caring arms of grandma. The latter carried the tiny little bundle of joy close to her chest as if she were some delicate eggs that must be shielded from breakage. This was a most precious egg indeed!

Oguebe the grandpa, walked more briskly ahead of the party so as to get to the car park. He needed to get the car warmed up for a few minutes for the benefit of the new baby. He also needed to get the car closer to the front of the hospital, so the baby would not have to be carried for a long distance in the cold weather. That morning was not a day for his usual persuading of Agesi to walk briskly to where the car was parked as a means of getting a most-needed physical exercise. Agesi was, that morning, doing her first duty as a dutiful grandmother to a lovely granddaughter. Grandpa's role in the care of the baby was not yet fully defined. All that was required of grandpa at that stage was to merely chauffeur the newborn baby and her parents safely down to the latter's Dorchester Apartment.

As the party of the new-born Baby Lydia, her two parents, grandma and grandpa entered the two-bedroom apartment that was to be home for the following four months, a unanimous chorus of "Welcome Baby Lydia" rented the air by all four adults to Lydia the new family member.

The welcome chorus sounded like it was pre-arranged.
All four adults used the same words
And all four uttered the words simultaneously

It looked as if a toast was being proposed for the new member.
And all were standing except the new member
And she that was being toasted appeared to understand.
She was the only member not standing.
No, she was quietly lying in grandma's loving arms.
Maybe she understood but could not speak.
There is no proof yet that little infants did not understand what was going on around them.
The fact of not responding with words did not necessarily imply inability to understand; at least to some degree.
Yes, the little infant who was fully, wrapped in green and red-stripped white cotton baby blanket, save for the face, was sleeping soundly in her grandmother's arms.
It was obvious that a new life-style was about to begin for all concerned. Certainly, a lot would for some time revolve around this youngest member of the household.
From the moment of her arrival it was obvious that the new little lady of the house was set to rewrite the rules. She might appear to be the weakest member of the family. But her influence on the status quo was undeniable. And everybody and everything would bend over backwards to conform with her wishes.

The heater in the living room on the first floor was turned low before the family members left for the hospital three days earlier. The room was consequently barely warm when the party returned with the new-born baby. It was certainly cooler than the car and the hospital environments before it warmed up some minutes later as the heating was increased.

As soon as the little lady of the house was placed on her crib, she made wriggling movements of disapproval. A shrill cry of "waaaa! waaaa! waaaa!" rented the air. The pitch and intensity of the cry belied the size of the creature which uttered the sound. But good a thing, the creature was a human person, a lovely human person, not one of those tiny birds which uttered cooing sounds deeper and louder than the miniature size of the avian which uttered the sounds from a nearby tree top.

Has any heard the tiny pigeon cooing from a nearby roof top?

Has any heard the sound of the little raven?

How does either sound compare in relativity of size and intensity with the sound of the large turkey or the long-legged desert ostrich?

If intensity of sound were to be the real measure of physical size, perhaps nobody would hear the cry of little babies. They are so tiny. Yet, they emit such shrill noises. Noises? No, not noises, but melodious attention-seeking sounds.

But just as the hood does not make the monk, the intensity of a baby's cry does not depict the size of the baby.

Little Baby Lydia had announced her presence by her shrill and loud cry.

At the onset of the shrill cry, both Nena and Agesi immediately and simultaneously stretched out their hands into the little bassinet within which Baby Lydia lay. Grandpa and grandma ought to have known better to check and warm up the crib before letting baby into it!

"She recognizes that the temperature has changed" Dave said.

"This is a little unusual. Many of them do not readily cry out at slight temperature changes at this stage", Agesi said.

"Baby Lydia is a little Big Girl, and so, don't be surprised that she knows when the temperature changes" Nena said, staring with profound admiration down into the bassinet at her little angel.

Soon, after the bassinet was warmed up, the crying ceased.

Then another round of swirling movements was followed by crying.

Oguebe was observing and learning. He had neither taken up, nor offered to take up any baby-sitting role yet.

But Dave would go back to South Africa soon. And Nena would have to concentrate on her studies if she must graduate. And of course, Agesi was in paid employment and could not manipulate her working hours from the times set out by her employers. It was only he, Oguebe who was in a position to take out time without permission from anybody.

And so, it was already obvious to Oguebe that care for Baby Lydia in those crucial early days was going to be a shared responsibility between him and his wife, Agesi.

As Oguebe ruminated, another shrill cry emanated from the little lady in the bassinet. She seemed to be getting more uncomfortable so soon after returning home.

Could she have sensed that there was some anticipated difficulty about her care?

Could she have overheard some discussions about the difficulty with procuring a baby-sitter for her?

"This time it is possible that she is wet. We have not changed her diapers since we left the hospital room", Agesi said.

The latter then proceeded to inspect Baby Lydia's diapers.

True to Agesi's suspicion, the little lady needed to have a diaper change.

The three-day leave of absence that Agesi had taken soon ended. She had to take the evening Peter-Pan last bus back to Sunderland. That way, she would be able to attend work the following morning. Oguebe whose schedule was a lot more flexible, being privately employed, stayed back in Boston.

Although Dave was around, he did not have a valid United States Drivers' License. And so, any little errands that needed transportation would in the interval, during Nena's puerperal period, be carried out by Oguebe. And Dave had taken off from his graduate studies and part-time job in Johannesburg for only two weeks. And the travel time would eat into those fourteen days.

The burden of unplanned baby-sitting was gravitating around Grandpa.

And the circumstances and Boston environment did not make for easy availability of house help or babysitter.

Stringent searches and numerous contacts were made but to no avail.

One thing alone was certain:

Little Baby Lydia must be catered for.

If she was hungry, she would cry

And if she was wet or uncomfortable by any degree, she would scream.

And her voice would send every adult scrambling to
offer reprieve.

She was another "She, who must be obeyed". Oguebe
had read an earlier similar title by Rider Haggard as a
High School text.

Where the care would come from or what planning
would go into ensuring it, was none of the little lady's
problems. It was something for the adults to worry
about.

Yet, she was so tiny.

And most of the time she lay apparently helpless on
her back.

She was not initially able to turn her neck.

But her hands and legs were highly mobile.

And her finger nails were as sharp as razor

And they were ever ready to be used.

And she would inflict dozens of nail scratch-marks
even on her own face.

What those nails could do to other peoples' faces
could only be imagined.

And those fingers and finger-nails were too tiny to be
readily visible.

They were barely accessible for trimming except with
magnifying glasses.

And any attempt to grab them for trimming were
fiercely resisted with every strength.

And so, tiny hand-gloves were placed over the lady's
fingers to protect her from herself.

She could only kick, scratch, eat, sleep, pee, cry and
poop.

And her little world appeared so limited to her
immediate surroundings.

Again, little Baby Lydia dominated her environment.
Her shrill cry kept everybody on his or her toes.
And even when her wishes were everybody's
command

those wishes were often vague or were very poorly
defined.
But they kept everybody guessing.
And everybody scrambled to satisfy her wishes, or
what those wishes were perceived to be.
Little Baby Lydia was not just a little princess, she
loomed larger than a powerful queen.

Neither mom nor dad nor grandma nor grandpa could
always guess it right.
No, none could always guess right, what a relentless
cry was indicative of.
But all were always sure of one thing that never
failed:
Little baby Lydia must always be attended to.
Again, her wishes were everybody's command.
Her displeasure indicated by a little shrill cry
brought sadness and apprehension to all and sundry.
And her gentle smile even when she smiled at
nothing,
or made involuntary smiling movements by the
parting of her lips,
made everybody smile and everybody would be
happy.

What little angel there was in Little Baby Lydia?
What fairy queen larger than life the little cherub was?
There was no doubt in anybody's mind
There was no gainsaying the truth that was manifest
on every face
That a happy Little Baby Lydia invariably made
everybody's day.

Chapter 5

DRIFT INTO UNPLANNED BABY-SITTING

Oguebe and Agesi while visiting Nena, occupied the single guest room on the second floor of Nena's rented Harbor Point Dorchester Apartment. Nena's master bedroom which contained Baby Julia's cot was also on the second floor while the kitchen and living rooms were on the first floor. The first three days after the discharge of the mother and child from hospital were apparently uneventful. The joy that pervaded the air was initially still too vibrant for anybody to feel the stresses of sleeplessness.
The lights in the master bedroom were switched on each time Oguebe woke up at the cry of the baby,
It looked as if Dave and Nena hardly ever slept at night.
The stress of sleeplessness after some days subsequently began to tell on the faces of the new parents.

Two days after Little Baby Lydia was discharged from the maternity ward, Oguebe saw how stressed Dave and Nena looked after keeping awake at night to observe the baby. He therefore offered to look after Baby Lydia for two nights from the early hours of the mornings.

This offer was in addition to helping with the baby part of the wakeful day. It was to enable the parents to catch some sleep. That way, the young parents would be able to withstand the near-continuous attention that the baby needed, even in the cot during the course of the day. That way the young and inexperienced parents would not break down from sleeplessness and fatigue. It was an innocuous offer of help that was at first not intended to last longer than a night or two. Little did Grandpa realize that, by his offer to help momentarily, he was inexorably setting the stage for an unplanned long-term baby-sitting.

"I will look after the baby from 4 in the mornings if you can transfer the cot to my room. Alternatively, you can procure a second cot and station it temporarily in my room. That way you two can catch some sleep so you remain strong enough to carry on with the day's wakefulness", Oguebe had volunteered. The offer was snatched on the spot and almost simultaneously by both parents.

"That would be excellent, Dad" Nena exclaimed with a sigh of relief.

"If you can do that, Sir, half of our problems in this regard would have been solved" Dave said almost simultaneously,

The ground was thus finally set for a new role for Grandpa as a babysitter.

This role was to get fully actualized after ten days when Dave had to travel back to his regular schedule in Johannesburg. The earlier plans to temporarily work in the USA so as to help with the care of the baby while the mother went to school had not materialized.

As of the time Dave departed back to Johannesburg there were no concluded plans in place for where Baby Lydia would stay while her mother went to school. The saving grace for the moment was that Grandpa being self-employed and thus capable of adjusting his schedules, could afford to put in some extra days with the new mother and her baby.

Dave's ten day visit to his fiancé and daughter had obviously been of great help to Nena and Baby Lydia. But he had to leave back to his base to continue with his research program.
There appeared to be no assurance about when Dave would be permanently back to be with his daughter again. It was Nena's wish that that would be pretty soon since the burden of single parenthood was not one that she had planned for.
"I had never bargained for single parenthood. And the idea of long-distance relationships had never been my wish." Nena said.
"I had always looked forward to a small but united family where each parent would contribute his or her quota in raising the children of the family" Nena said.

Little Baby Lydia was completely oblivious of the failed arrangements and alternative plans that were being made for her care and upkeep. She was either asleep, or was feeding or was crying most of the time. On the few occasions when she would be seen with her two eyes open she would be kicking or stretching her tiny hands and legs. The black of the rounded eye-balls were all that were usually visible and indeed only barely visible. The white conjunctiva was almost always hidden. And she could stare on an object for minutes on end without blinking.

She was averse to bright light and would immediately shut her eyes tightly whenever the lights were suddenly turned on.

As Nena was home nursing her baby, the other medical students in her class were very busy putting finishing touches to their studies. They were completing their patient requirements prior to their degree conferment.
Nena's classmates were however very gracious. They came in batches to visit Nena and Little Baby Lydia. They brought various items of gifts ranging from baby's garments to baby's bath tub, to babies' shoes, stockings and toys.
Tessy, Nena's closest friend brought assorted gifts and visited frequently to intimate Nena with developments in the course so that the latter would not feel completely "lost" or overwhelmed on her resumption of classes.

"Don't worry Nena, you will catch up with the rest of the class as soon as you resume back at school. No doubt a lot is going on. There is a final scramble for patients, but I will hand over my excess patients over to you. Many of our other classmates are also eager to help. With your great academic capability and your hard work, you will catch up", Tessy told Nena.
"I know it is going to be tough, Tessy, but I will try my best", Nena replied.
"I am very happy and very delighted with my new role as a mother" Nena further said.
"But it is my ardent wish to graduate with my classmates."
Tessy was obviously getting worried about whether her friend Nena was considering deferring her graduation year for full time baby-care. Her fears were greatly allayed by Nena's response and determination.

It was obvious that a final decision about how to care for the baby needed to be taken and very urgently too if Nena would achieve her educational ambition. Renewed searches were made about Day Care facilities which would take in Little Baby Lydia. All but one of the searches proved abortive. All suitable centers were already full. Some others would not take babies in Baby Lydia's age group. Most facilities accepted babies who were at least six months of age. Baby Lydia was only two weeks old when Nena considered going back to classes.

Some other facilities would not accept babies whose two parents were not available to sign the forms. Others charged outrageously-high fees with other very unfavorable conditions like having one of the parents as a staff of the institution that owned the facility. Many day care facilities were attached to large institutions and catered primarily to children of their staff members with only very few spots for outsiders. They indicated boldly on their application forms: "For staff children and staff dependents only".

Baby Lydia seemed to be disadvantaged all round. None of her parents was working in Boston. And the facility owned by the institution which Nena attended was easily filled up. Apparently, they did not expect that students would be making babies while in school.

At the end the searches boiled down to only one private facility. The lone facility that still had its doors open was a private facility which was run by a late-middle-aged lady who operated alone in her one bed-room apartment.

On being contacted over the phone the proprietress said that she would admit babies from new-born to five years.

"I still get space if you can come down now, now!" the lady said on phone.

The lady's English was not very intelligible, but that was not the issue at that time.

All that mattered to Nena and her parents was that they were able to secure a place that would accept their baby for day-care so that Nena could get back to school and graduate with her class mates.

"I am very happy and excited that we have found a place which will accept Baby Lydia here in Boston." Nena exclaimed.

"But you don't yet know the conditions, Nena." Agesi said.

"Conditions, mom? Is it the conditions of the place or the conditions that they will give us for accepting the baby?" Nena asked looking her mom anxiously in the face.

"Both, Nena. But more particularly the conditions in the place. You will not like to leave your baby in a pig's sty, would you?"

"It's true, mom, but there is hardly any condition that cannot improve given the necessary supervision and instructions by the parents", Nena insisted, looking obviously very triumphant with her search.

"Well, I am equally thrilled at our securing a place. But we must not smile too soon until we see the place and discuss with the management. Very often, what you see is not what you get." Agesi stated.

Oguebe listened as his wife and daughter argued about a facility which they had not seen. He appeared to be in no mood to contribute to the discussions. All that appeared to bother him was his wish that a good daycare facility be secured for his granddaughter and for him to get back as soon as was possible to his house and business in Sunderland.

The following morning after they received the phone number of the "facility" Agesi called back the place to ascertain the conditions for enrollment and the possibility of booking an appointment. Agesi was hoping that she would perhaps speak with a more refined staff-member in the facility as different from the person who she spoke with the previous day.
The call was however picked up by the same lady who Agesi had spoken with the previous day, as shown by the voice of the person who answered the call.
The lady who took the call spoke pidgin English a mixture of English, Spanish and Portuguese, a language which was popular in many parts of West Africa and parts of the Caribbean Islands.

The lady announced that she was readily available to accept Baby Lydia immediately.
After Agesi had introduced herself over the phone, the lady immediately replied.
"I speak with you yesterday and I say make you bring the baby immediately. I tell you, say, I still get space." The lady rattled over the phone as if in a prepared speech.
In order to be sure that the age of the baby was not going to be a barrier against enrollment, Agesi asked:
"Our baby is only four weeks old and I hope that you accept babies in that age group."
Without hesitation the lady at the other end immediately replied:
"Yes, just bring the pikin!"
"Did you say pigeon?" Agesi asked. She did not quite understand the lady.
"I say, make you just bring the pikin"
Agesi still did not quite understand what the lady said that she should bring.
She switched the volume to loud speaker and asked again,

"Kindly send me a text message and state specifically what you need us to bring along."
At that point, Nena who was sitting by the edge of the bed by her mom, took over the phone from her mother and said:
"Hello, my name is Nena. I am the mother of the baby. Please give us an appointment. And what are the things that you said that we should bring."
The lady again stated
"My name be Elizabeth, Madam Elizabeth Kokoro. But them de call me Mama Titi. So, you can call me Mama Titi. Appointment no necessary for my Day Care. Just bring the pikin. I de care well-well, for all kinds of small pikin. Even day-old pikin, I go take for my place."
"Why did she say we should bring the pigeon?" Nena, asked, ostensibly angry that the lady was referring to her baby as a pigeon.
Agesi and Oguebe were quite familiar with the word "pikin" which meant "little child" in the pidgin English spoken widely in the part of West Africa from where they originally came. Nena was however not familiar with that word. It was only during the clarification from Madam Elizabeth Kokoro, alias Mama Titi, that Agesi explained to Nena that the lady was saying "pikin", and not pigeon.

By 10 am the following morning Nena, Grandpa and Grandma set out for Mama Titi's supplied address with Baby Lydia in her detachable cot to be attached to the car's back seat.
As the GPS took the visitors further towards the rather non-hospitable neighborhood of Quincy, a suburb of Boston Massachusetts, the countenance of the visitors began to change. Finally, the destination was reached.

The vicinity of the multiple apartment building was littered with newspapers and debris. The building, even in spite of a new coat of paint on the exterior walls, was looking every inch thoroughly run down. The filthy condition of the elevator that took the visitors to Mama Titi's stipulated fifth floor appointment was most unwelcome. A very bulky vicious-looking heavily-tattooed young man who entered the elevator simultaneously with Nena and her mother and baby, was a source of great worry for Nena until the man disembarked on the 3rd floor. Nena's worry stemmed from the man's non-response to a courtesy defensive greeting which Nena had extended to the man when the latter entered the elevator. The man simply looked at the baby in the cot and swiftly turned away his face as if the sight of an infant nauseated him. He thereafter had broken into a wild noisy song which he continued on, until he disembarked from the elevator.

For the short time that the man was in the elevator, Nena imagination pictured one of the scary stories of elevator strangulation that she had read of in the past.

The graffiti on the walls of the elevator were even more scary. More sources of worry were to surface. In response to the door-bell in front of the stipulated Apartment # 504C, a pleasant-talking, bespectacled late middle-aged lady with loud perfume and heavy make-up, welcomed the visitors into her apartment. The fresh smell of sprayed air fresheners did not quite camouflage the mousy odor from many untidy bundles of clothing that were rolled up at virtually every available space in the living room. It was very obvious that the good lady must have tried her best to tidy up her apartment and had tried her best to impress her visitors and possible future customers.

Four children aged between two and three years were playing around some toys that littered around the room. Each of the poor little kids had running nose even when they appeared happy and well-dressed. Each had some toys with which they were playing on the rather filthy worn-out floor carpet.

A baby's cot with freshly-made linen wedged behind the door and prevented the latter from opening fully. Six baby's play pans with many baby's toys within them, were taking up much-needed space at the further end of the relatively small living room.

"Welcome to our happy home" Mama Titi announced beaming with smiles. She had many missing posterior teeth which were very obvious when the lady laughed. A set of poorly-maintained and improperly-fitting removable dentures anteriorly completed the evidence of poor dental attention. Behind the good lady's photochromic bifocal eye glasses that were supported by greatly-worn out frames, were eyeballs that however still radiated grace and a determination to succeed in making a living.

"I get four pikin now. Sometimes I get up to six. Boston mothers all of them like me because I charge only small money to look after small pikin. I charge only twenty dollar per day for one small pikin from morning till night No late collection fee. But you go bring baby formula, your baby food, any type of food except dry fish or fish with bones. Also, you go bring diapers and baby clothes."

Mama Titi was brisk and concise with her terms. It was amazing how precise and resolute she was even in spite of her poor English and her graceful advancing years.

Mama Titi was also very observant of the physiognomy of her clients. She looked Agesi in the face and was quick to observe that the latter wore a rather frowning look of disapproval. She quickly added.

"Madam, you no look too happy. But you be my sister. All women who come from Africa, them all be my sister. See, all my pikins, them happy. You want make I make you small coffee?

"You see, when my children are happy, I too be happy. But when them no happy, or when them cry too much, I take cloth tie them for my back like we do for my country in Africa. Soon them go sleep for my back, no problem. That time I go become happy."

Then, as if to demonstrate how happy her resident-children were, Mama Titi picked up a toy from the floor and shook it vigorously in front of the youngest of the little children playing on the floor.

True to Mama Titi's words, the little girl of about two years beamed a smile as she grabbed the toy from Mama Titi.

"Make you say "Thank you.""

And immediately the little girl responded

"Thank you, ma'am."

Mama Titi immediately reached for a candy bar from a glass jar on the shelf and rewarded the little girl.

Another "Thank you ma'am" followed the little gift as the other three residents, two boys and one girl, all looked up to see whether they too would get candies.

"No worry, guys, you will get yours later," Madam Titi assured her wards.

It was a great advertisement for a facility which otherwise had little to recommend it.

The two boys giggled in approval as Mama Titi rubbed the neatly-plaited hair of the second little girl.

Agesi bent forwards over the prize-winning little girl and the latter beamed a pleasant smile at Agesi. Those were truly very pleasant little children. And it was obvious that Mama Titi was very close with them.

It was a very favorable demonstration even when the obvious disapproval of the facility was demonstrated on Nena's face.
Meanwhile Little Baby Lydia, who had woken up from sleep gazed steadily at the four little children.
Could she be wondering if she was going to be one of them? Certainly, her imagination had not reached to that extent. But certainly, hardly anybody knew for certain how intelligent little babies were. There might be a false assessment of their intelligence because of their inability to vocalize their thoughts. Perhaps they knew far more than adults could imagine.

Mama Titi was very hospitable. She pulled up a nearby chair and dusted it up with the palm of her right hand. She then cleaned the dusty hand with the palm of the other hand and offered the chair to Agesi who was carrying Baby Lydia in her mobile cot.

"Make you sit down Madam. Carrying little babies in cots, it be big job. Me, I de carry baby for more than fifty years now. I carry all the eight children which I born for myself before I come de carry the children of my children here for America. I come for this country eighteen years ago to baby-sit my granddaughter. I come end up baby-sitting three other babies for my daughter. After that, I come gain big experience for baby-sitting. That one come teach me well, well, and I come begin my own business of privately looking after babies when them mothers go work or school. Some of my babies now don become big boys and big girls. Even though I no get certificate or government license, I get plenty experience for nursing private babies", Mama Titi said triumphantly.

What Mama Titi lacked in formal education, facilities and hospitable environment, she made up for, with politeness, pleasant words and excellent public relations.
But the unsuitability of the facility was unmistakable to Nena, Agesi and Oguebe. Even though some mothers entirely trusted their babies to her care, Mama Titi's day-care facility, in Nena's view, was without doubt below standard.
But Mama Titi nonetheless exuded confidence and sincerity in her facility as she confidently added:

"I no need you to fill big forms. I no need even deposit. Just bring your pikin for morning or night and when you want to collect him back, just pay me twenty dollars, finish. My own is easy. It no be like all those big places with big gates, big grammar and big fees. For this place it be direct supervision and your baby go get sense well-well. I get home-made PhD for to make small pikin get native intelligence. My only regret it be say, I no speak good Spanish. But Spanish mothers them trust me well-well. These pikin you see here them speak English and Spanish. I want make I go school learn small Spanish. That way I go get many more Spanish mothers to bring them children here. Even now, I speak small-small Spanish. Signor and Signora be the first Spanish words that I learnt. I try to learn one new Spanish word every day. The trouble be say, I learn one new word and forget one old one. But I still go try." Mama Titi said.

Even in spite of their skepticism Agesi and Nena could not but admire the honest and enduring efforts being made by Mama Titi.
"You are trying very hard, Mama Titi" Agesi said trying to be of encouragement.
"Yes, I try small-small. The problem it be that when I learn one word for Tuesday, I come forget the one which I learn for Monday. But, no problem, I try small- small", Mama Titi said, beaming with smiles and displaying her brilliantly-white but poorly-fitting anterior dentures.

Mama Titi exuded confidence. She obviously meant well. But it was certainly not the type of day-care that her visitors wanted for Little Baby Lydia.
The visiting party put up a smiling face and thanked Mama Titi profusely as they made to leave.

"Thank you for your time, Madam Titi ..." Agesi started.
But Mama Titi immediately corrected her:
"No, it no be Madam Titi, it be Mama Titi. Titi. It be the name which them de call my small daughter when she was small. She be big girl now. Na her daughter I first come America come, do babysitter. Titi, she be big girl now and she work for that big bank near Boston University Medical Center."
"Sorry, Mama Titi, we will go now. We will consider our options and get back to you." Agesi told Mama Titi at the end of the visit.

Mama Titi was also a very generous woman and she remained pleasant to the end.
As the visitors were about to leave, she pulled open a drawer from a nearby table and offered a big pack of chocolate to each of the three adult visitors. Then she offered a fourth one specially to Nena.
"Make you take this extra one for my little pikin so you go get make more milk for her before I see you again. If you no want come, please make you help direct other people make them bring them pikins here. I de look after pikins well-well."

It was a most cordial reception and with an even more cordial ending.
It would not matter if the parties were not to see again.
As the visitors waited for the elevator, Nena could not help sharing her anxiety, not of the facility, but of their former co-passenger in the elevator.
"I hope we don't again encounter the burly young man that we rode this elevator earlier with" Nena said.
"That was exactly what was in my mind as we stepped out of Madam Titi's apartment", Agesi said.

"But the fellow was just one man. There was no way he could have overpowered the three of us in the elevator if it came to a struggle" Oguebe said.

"You mean the four of us" Nena said, looking jokingly at Little baby Lydia.

"Oh, I forgot there was a fourth powerful young lady here", Oguebe said.

"Yes, Little baby Lydia can at least cry loudly and attract attention.

"You never should underestimate the power of little babies", Agesi said, laughing.

On their way back from Mama Titi's facility, Agesi and Nena exhaustively discussed their opinions about what they witnessed.

"What is your general opinion about the place, mom?" Nena asked her mother.

"I saw the expression on your face while we were with Mama Titi, Nena, and I share your opinion even without your expressing it."

"But supposing I tell you that my opinion is that of approval, mom?" Nena joked.

"Then I will know that it may be time to start consulting a shrink!"

Agesi said.

"You know this condition that psychiatrists call Post-partum psychosis?"

"Wow, mom, don't even go there. After the first seventy-two hours of sleeplessness following Baby Lydia's birth, my head was like swimming and swollen and the first thought that came into my mind was whether I was going to have post-partum psychosis. It was only after you and dad started looking after the baby from the early hours of the morning that I started regaining my composure." Nena said.

"Well, we thank God that we did not have to call in the shrinks to help shrink the swollen brain." Agesi said. "And so, back again to Mama Titi's facility. I appreciate her zeal and great efforts at caring for babies. But the environment is certainly not the type of place that I would love to entrust my baby." Nena said.

"But those her babies can still grow to be stars in this country, you never can tell."

"True, mom, but you never can tell what long-term harm a filthy environment can bring to little children."

"A filthy environment can also help confer immunity; don't you think so?"

"Ha, ha, ha, but we don't immunize babies with dirt so they develop immunity, do we?"

Before the discussion and jokes could go any further, Baby Lydia started kicking and crying. The party had to hurry up to enter the car to pacify the Little lady who appeared to be protesting an unnecessary and protracted discussion about her care.

Mama Titi called twice in the following three days but after the second missed call Nena called her back and politely thanked her. She further informed her that she had changed her plans and would want to care for the baby at home by herself for some time.

Mama Titi took the loss of clientele better than anticipated.

"No problem, Ma'am. Any time you are ready, I be ready to have your lovely pikin. You go be happy when she comes here," Mama Titi added confidently. She was very confident about her facility and did not display any disappointment about the apparent disapproval of her day-care facility.

"Nobody would wish to hurt the ego of an amiable lady like Mama Titi. Certainly, nobody would want to diminish the enormity of her love for children or her determination to be of some use to society. That was obvious even in the face of the shortcomings of her substandard and unregistered Day Care facility." Agesi said.

If there was anybody who would not attempt to diminish Mama Titi, it was Nena. Much as she did not give a pass to the facility, she still greatly appreciated Mama Titi and she sent the latter a Thank You card shortly after the visit. And, in response to Mama Titi's missed calls, she enclosed some presents and thanking her for her hospitality during their visit. Mama Titi called back and was full of appreciation.

"Mama Titi is obviously a very industrious lady. If she had a little more education, she certainly would have been a great business entrepreneur." Agesi said.
"But not many people would wish to expose their little babies to such hazardous conditions as we witnessed in Mama Titi's private children's nursery especially at Baby Lydia's tender age." Nena said.

Chapter 6

RE-LEARNING THE ART OF DIAPER CHANGING

With the failure of the search for a Day Care facility for Baby Lydia, it became obvious that Nena would need to suspend her studies and her graduation to stay at home to look after her baby. The alternative was that one of her parents would sacrifice their work to temporarily baby-sit the baby until a facility was found for her.

The available options were again re-enumerated. Nena was in school. Grandma was in paid employment and would not be as available as required if she must keep her job. The least disruptive was that Grandpa who operated a small private business would have to take some time off his small business to look after the baby. It was an option that Grandpa had not prepared for, or even thought of. But the situation on the ground was akin to one of make-or-break. Grandpa and Grandma each wanted Nena to succeed in her academics. At the same time, they did not want Little Baby Lydia to suffer any family-care deprivation. It was a situation that Grandpa had not even for a moment, fully bargained for.

But the major problem with the viable option was that Grandpa had never catered to the domestic needs of any baby. Even when Nena was growing up, Oguebe and Agesi had babysitters who lived in and who took complete charge of the baby in the absence of their mother. Grandpa had often seen diapers being changed. But he had never changed any by himself. He had seen babies being breast fed or bottle fed, but he had never bottle-fed any baby. He had indeed never had cause to change the baby's clothing or indeed carry any infant in his arms for any length of time. It was that strange to him.

But it was imperative this time around, that Grandpa would play a role that would involve all the above, from diaper-changing to bottle-feeding to laundering, to baby-rocking and more, and fully too. And these were to be in his latter stages in life.

Grandpa was almost at the stage when some unlucky grandpas would have to start using and changing their own diapers. A few less lucky ones would have started forgetting a thing or two.

Again, chances were that the fingers might no longer be very steady.

Supposing Grandpa tripped while carrying the baby? Supposing his eyes got dimmed and he stepped on the baby while the latter lay on her back while playing with her big toe on the floor carpet?

When the baby cried repeatedly and refused the feeding bottle, and pushed away anything and everything that got close to her mouth, would grandpa, even with his medical background, be in a good position to decipher what it was that was hurting the baby?

Would he have the patience and the technique to carry the baby and very gently rock her and sing her to sleep?

Would grandpa be able to memorize those nursery rhythms with which he would pacify the baby. Could he recite some soothing songs?
Would he have the patience and the tenderness to rub the baby's back gently till she fell asleep again?
These were little tricks which nature appeared to have bestowed on the gentle palms of mothers and grandmothers. At least, so it was believed in the culture from which Oguebe and Agesi hailed.

Would one dozen or more years in America have helped infuse the art of infant nursing into a male senior citizen who had never practiced the art of baby-sitting before in his life?
No, those arts appeared to be bestowed by Nature only on her female creations.
But, yes, the determination to learn and apply, were strong in Oguebe even if the experience was poor or non-existent.
And Oguebe was doubly lucky. He did not suffer from any of the illnesses or other debilitating diseases that tended to be associated with aging. His vision was good and his hearing was sharp. His wants were small and his attitude to life was that of complete simplicity and giving. And both his spirit and his body were strong and resolute. And he was determined to see that his daughter Nena graduated on schedule. He was resolute on his wife Agesi's job not being disrupted. And in the midst of these, he would entertain nothing which would compromise his granddaughter Little Baby Lydia's well-being and her being lovingly catered for, in her most crucial years in life.

Yes, with Baby Lydia's biological father Dave back to Johannesburg, and Agesi back to her job after a total of three weeks intermittent leave of absence, and with Nena about to restart classes and clinics after staying away from for nearly four weeks, it was time to take major decisions about Baby Lydia's upkeep and care. Would it be better to keep Baby Lydia in Boston at least for a few hours of tender care from her mother daily?

Or, would it be too much of a distraction for Nena who was at a critical stage in her studies?

And, the latter part of Nena's studies was pure clinical work that required her physical presence and active participation, if she must graduate on schedule.

Or, would it be better for the baby to move down to Sunderland with Grandpa and Grandma, perhaps to be seen and attended to by her mother only at alternate weekends?

Staying back in Boston even if it be in a separate room from her mother would still be a distraction for Nena, albeit a joyful distraction.

Baby Lydia would still cry at night when she was wet. She would still cry in a shrill voice when she was uncomfortable for any reasons.

She would still cry for reasons which only the prying eyes or intuitive thoughts of a mother could detect.

Certainly, Baby Lydia would still cry for no obvious reasons, or for a variety of reasons all of which would be ascribed to "intestinal colic" for want of a better or more accurate diagnosis.

And every cry would attract Nena's attention.

A mother would never plug off her ears with ear buds at the cry of her baby.

No, she would not shut off her attention from her loving baby, no matter how hard she tried.

"I once suggested that you brought the baby's cot permanently to my room so that you could sleep a little better at night1" Oguebe had advised.

"No, dad, I will cope. I cannot afford to hear even the slightest sound of her cry from your room and keep quiet or feel at ease" Nena said.

"And if Baby Lydia moved down to Sunderland with your mom and me, would you be able to sleep better and keep off the phone at night?" Oguebe asked her daughter.

"I will be on the phone every moment of the day that I am not in class or in the clinics. And even at night, I may call even in my dreams." Nena told her dad.

Grandpa knew that it was a moment of decision. He got on the phone and had a very long discussion with Agesi who had traveled early that morning back to western Massachusetts.

At the end of the lengthy discussions between husband and wife, a decision was reached: Grandpa would have to learn a new mini-trade. He would have to take a long leave off his small private literary business and stay back in Boston. He would have to be a full-time babysitter for Baby Lydia at least for a couple of months if Grandma must not lose her job and if the baby's mom must graduate!

The hands of Grandpa must learn new arts, the art of carrying and pacifying a baby, even at his latter stages of life.

And so Oguebe settled down to a family volunteer job. It was a major role reversal; a labor of love at the utmost.

A few days of watching Agesi change the baby's diapers were tutorials enough.

On the first few days a few mistakes were made. The diapers were either too tight or they were too loose as Nena would counsel. Luckily, the elastic on the diapers was specially designed. Nena too was initially a novice, but she learnt fast enough. A mother did not appear to spend half as much time on the tutorials as a Grandpa would spend. The natural instinct of a mother must be playing a part.

The changing of the dress was the difficult part. The subject appeared so tiny and so fragile that she was difficult to handle.
A lot of the dresses un-zipped or un-buttoned through and through for ease of changing; thank goodness! The few that needed to be slipped across the head were the biggest nightmares.
The neck could not hold the head steady and the latter easily swung backwards.
A forward drop when stabilizing the head with the palm of the hand was even more alarming.
"Good god, it was easy to forget that the one-month-old baby could not yet hold the neck!
The palm of the hand needed to support at the same time the head, the neck and the upper back.
Who ever knew that infants could be so tiny?
Who knew that their heads were so wobbly?
"Could the human person be so weak, so initially fragile, intellectually blank and so helpless, and still claim to be Homo sapiens, the epitome of the mammalian ladder?" Oguebe soliloquized.

Yes, Grandpa once in a while forgot that the baby could not hold her neck. The immediate forward or backward drop of the highly-mobile neck was inevitably a warning.

"Oh my God, let no damage occur to the neck or spine from this drop!"

It always looked as if the neck would snap if the head was not immediately supported.

But Grandpa remembered fast that the head unsupported, would drop forwards or backwards.

His own pediatric postings, though four decades in the past, coupled with his transient general practice experience must be called fast into play.

The day-old lamb would stand after a couple of hours of birth.

The newly-hatched chick would stand up within hours after breaking free from the egg.

Even the goat by which name a man was ridiculed if he behaved foolishly, stood on its own within hours of birth.

But the one-month-old Homo sapiens would not be able to hold his or her neck for months after its birth!

There, the human infant lay, "mewling and pucking in the nurse's arms", as William Shakespeare would say.

Thanks to the well-developed cerebral hemisphere of man!

He would otherwise have been easy prey to the many other animals whom he derogatorily referred to as "lower animals".

And so, Grandpa learnt to spread his long thin fingers from the back of the head to the back of the shoulders of month-old Baby Lydia.

And the subject was so tiny that one half of the entire body would be supported on the palm of Grandpa's hand.

And what was left of the rest of the body was not too large to miss.

What Grandpa could not learn was how to bathe the baby. The preparations for the bathe were perhaps too elaborate for him. The plastic baby-bath-tub was the first and the largest of the armamentarium. Mixing of the water to required temperature was no easy task. The baby-soap, the cloth bathing sponge and other paraphernalia like cups would be handy. Assembling the necessary gadgets was quite a task.

Stabilizing the tiny fragile-looking creature, the youngest member of the growing human family was the biggest nightmare.

But little Baby Lydia was quite a pleasure to observe. She was expected to protest when bathed with the temperature-titrated water.

The bathing did not involve routine pouring of water as adults would do.

It was more of wiping of the body with mild soap and cloth.

Pouring of water over the head was a taboo.

Mistake of water on the face would stir immediate gasp-like movements as if the baby would choke.

And wiping of the silky hair on the head must be done with caution.

Any excess water on the bathing cloth must be adequately squeezed off for certain.

And the eyes and nostrils of the little angel must be guarded with care

Wiping her face with damp warm towel always elicited a shrill cry.

It did not matter that the temperature of the water was carefully and suitably titrated.

If the water was a little too cold hell might appear to have been let loose.

And if the temperature was a little too hot it was a call to disaster.

Bathing the baby was thus a job for another
reincarnated and well-tutored Grandpa.
A baby's bath was more interesting to watch than a
task to be performed
It was an arduous task but the aftermath: a clean
little angel was worth all the care.
The lotion and the combed hair produced a baby that
was adorable to behold.

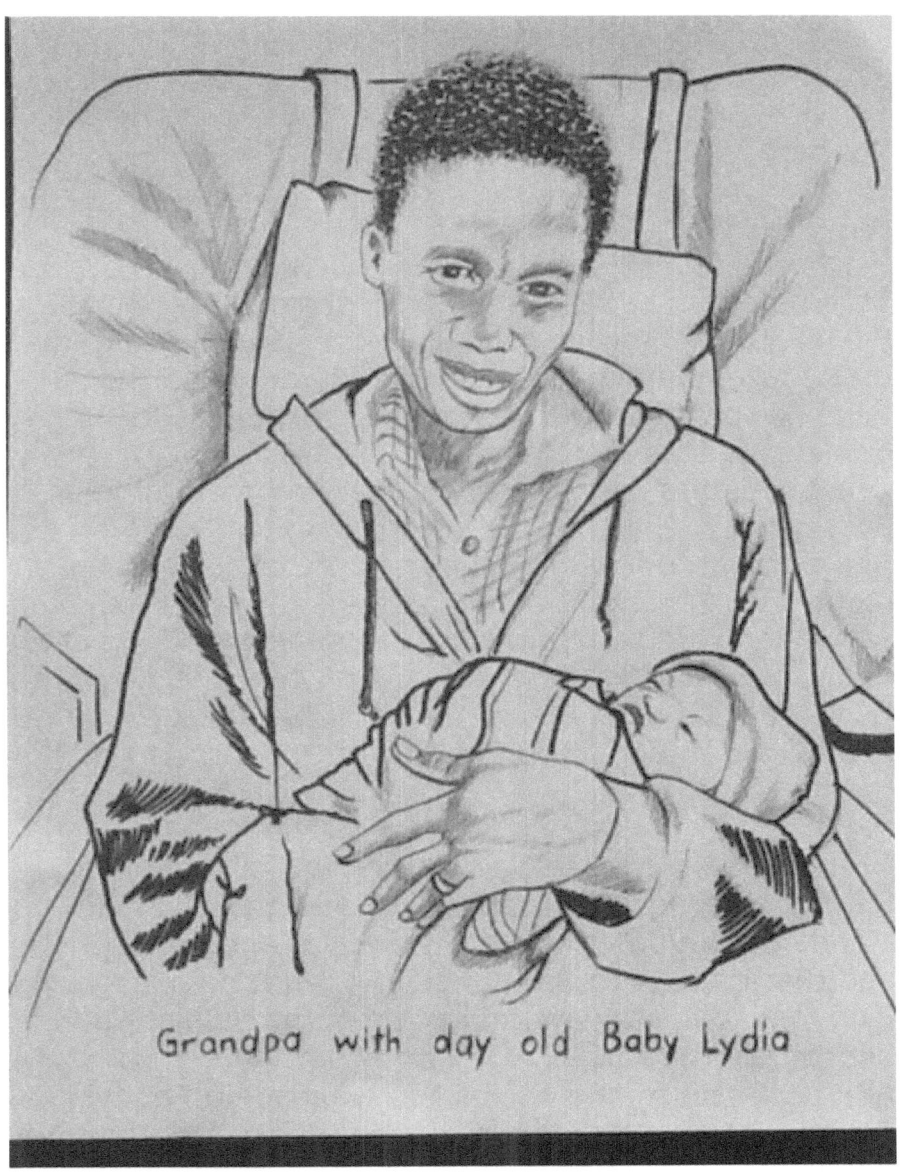

Grandpa with day old Baby Lydia

Chapter 7

BABY LYDIA MATURES BY THE DAY

Three months appeared to be an eternity.
Even with the joys of beholding Baby Lydia, each day
that passed appeared longer than twenty-four hours.
Tending to the baby's needs whether he was feeding
or sleeping was quite a task.
One needed to be eagle-eyed every moment of each
passing day.
Apart from the few interrupted hours of quiet sleep at
night, every moment of the remaining twenty fours
was laden with watchfulness. The supine position and
the activities of the little lady even when she slept
kept the supervising adult on his or her toes.
Even while asleep Little Baby Lydia appeared to rule
the house.

Grandma would leave Boston straight for work in
Springfield Massachusetts by Peter Pan Bus early
Monday morning. It was a distance of about 80 miles
and the first bus to Springfield must not be missed.
For a while Monday mornings appeared as nightmares
because of the rush.
And at the close of work on the succeeding Friday
Grandma would travel straight from work back to
Boston.
Grandpa was temporarily settled in Boston as the
emergency amateur in-house baby-sitter. And Nena
the embattled mother would keep awake a good part
of the night to pump breast milk. Thereafter she
would breastfeed Baby Lydia at intervals of about
three hours.

Nena would wake up at the slightest cry or audible turning of the baby. She easily heard such movement even from a distance of more than twenty feet and from a different room. She would lie in bed surrounded by piles of pending school assignments and with recorded gadgets of lectures and discussion groups stuck to her ears with ear phones.

Yes, Nena had all the cooperation from her classmates. She had full encouragement and all assurances of support from the parents around her. But, even with the latter, the obvious evidence of stress was written all over Nena.

"We are here to support you, Nena. You must take things a little easier so that you do not break down" Agesi regularly assured.

"Mom, you said you had me while in school? How did you cope with the enormous workload of school and baby-care?" Nena asked.

"Yes, honey, but the times were different. These are new times."

"How different? Did you get concessions from the school on some courses?"

"No, not at all. But I was younger. I just turned twenty-two when I had you. When you are that young, sometimes you don't appreciate the dangers and so, the stress is less.

Besides my age, I also had a lot of help from family and friends. My own mother, that is your grandmother, took off time from her work and stayed two full months with me. And I had two full time house helps. And the only duties of the house-helps were solely to look after you. They took turns to look after you. Moreover, your dad though also a student, was around me to lend support."

"How were you able to pay for all that, Mom?"

"That was in our native African setting. The house helps were not paid, at least not directly. They were volunteer relatives and friends of the family who sacrificed some years of school work to help their relations to raise kids."

"Those were major sacrifices indeed."

"Yes, but it was the culture of our people. It was rotatory. The girls took it in turns. Your aunties would do it for you, and you would be expected to do it for your own nephews and nieces.

I also was a baby-sitter for some of your aunties while they were babies. I did baby-sitting for three years for the children of my eldest cousin, the one you call "auntie Christina". That was why I did not start morning school until I was eight years old. I attended evening schooling which lasted only some four hours a day. There were two streams of schools: the morning stream which lasted from 8AM to 2PM. Then there was the afternoon stream which lasted from 2.30PM to 6.30PM for those children who could not attend the morning stream.

Baby-sitting was done by older children sometimes as young as six years for much younger children. I was lucky thereafter that I had acceleration in two classes in school. Those compensated for the years that I lost doing baby-sitting."

"Really?" Nena interjected in absolute surprise.

"But times have changed. Hardly any service is free these days, not even from close relatives." Agesi told Nena.

"From your narrative, Mom, times have really changed a lot. These are new times. I hope they are for the better." Nena said.

"But you should consider yourself lucky, Nena. What would you have done with your baby at this tender stage if your dad did not offer to baby-sit for you?"

"I probably would have dropped off momentarily from my studies!"

"Or you would have had to drop off your baby with Mama Titi."

"No, Mom, dropping off Baby Lydia with Mama Titi would not have been an option for me."

"Why not, if there were no alternatives?"

"No, not after we visited the place and I saw the condition of Mama Titi's house where the babies stayed. There was no way that I would have dropped off my baby there for day care. It was a harbinger of disease and ill health. I really felt sorry for those little kids that we saw there even though they appeared to look happy playing on the filthy carpet."

"But the kids were there with Mama Titi, and they have not become ill with filth-induced diseases."

"Mom, did you see how miserable those adorable little kids were looking? Did you see a lasting smile from any of their faces? I felt so much for those four little kids. But I did not wish to appear to be scornful or unappreciative of Mama Titi and her endeavors to do her best. She was certainly a very courteous and hardworking lady. It was the best that she knew. But, it certainly was not good enough."

"I agree with you, Nena. But Nature has a way of making up for deficiencies. Like I once said, any of those kids can still grow up to become a leader in this country. You never know."

"I don't doubt it Mom, but a good head-start in life is very often an advantage. Otherwise why did you once get private teachers for me to give me extra coaching at home after my regular school hours? I surely had the necessary head-start, didn't I?"

"As always, Nena, you win! But remember that it is not everybody who had the so-called head-start that does well in life. And, it does not mean that if one does not have a head-start, then the person would not do well in life."

And so, the conversation that never seemed to end went on between Nena and her mom.

Yes, the parents were there to support Nena. But the bulk of outstanding school work and skipped assignments lay squarely on the latter's shoulders. Her patients for her clinical requirements were not issues that any family members would be able to solve for her. She would have to satisfy her requirements otherwise she would have an extension. The responsibility lay squarely with her. Care for Baby Lydia was big but pleasant load for Nena. But school work was one bigger burden, a distasteful one.

Oguebe counted the days as he slowly learnt what it looked like to stay with a tiny little infant for many hours at a stretch. Nena often left the house before 8 AM each day. If she did not have patients booked in the clinic she would have discussion groups. And if she did not have discussion groups she would have practical classes in the labs.

Grandpa and Grandma on the other hand had their roles squarely cut out for them. And for Grandpa, at least for the moment, the role was purely and simply to baby-sit Little Baby Lydia.

It was a complete family role reversal, one that Oguebe had never envisaged, never prepared for, and indeed was not truly equipped for. No, he had not in his wildest of imaginations envisaged this. But when the challenge came up, he non-grudgingly braced up and played same with humility, equanimity and great joy.

He was clumsy at first. It was so boring for one who had been living a very exciting and active life. But after the first week it became more excitement, the grandpa having learnt to roughly differentiate the cries for hunger from the cries for wetness.
Every moment of staying with Little Baby Lydia was so fulfilling that it was difficult to realize that the days were rolling by.

The weeks appeared to go by very quickly. However, no serious working from home by Oguebe was possible; no, not with a tiny little baby who could wake up at any time and start crying.
Listening to cable news used to excite Oguebe greatly, especially when there were international news items that were of great socio-political significance.
But Oguebe was soon to find that the same news no matter how significant, lost its flavor when listened to again and again. He was a great lover of Cable News Network, and a number of other networks even before he immigrated to the United States. He was later to also find the ABC morning news and some aspects of the local news particularly interesting. With time, he came to appreciate the great significance of many other news and entertainment networks. Back in his Sunderland home in western Massachusetts he used to crave for time to spend on some of those networks. That was before he settled temporarily in Boston as an emergency baby-sitter. He began to have too much time on his hands but it was all intermittently-truncated time, invariably truncated by the cry or persistent kicking of a tiny little baby in a cot.
And the news and programs started getting boring. Within one month of his sojourn in Boston. Oguebe had become very familiar with the regular signature tunes of many routine programs.

He even began to hum some of the signature tunes like "Good Morning America", "New Day" and many others regular programs in different news channels.

Often at the point when Oguebe savored an on-going program the high-pitched cry of the baby would emanate from the cot. It soon became necessary often to lower the volume, or to turn off the TV or to mute it so the baby would not be awakened. As soon as the baby woke up, it would be bye-bye to any listening or to meaningful work on the computer. It would become impossible to listen to the program for the rest of the day or until the baby slept again.

Chapter 8.

MASTERING THE ART OF BABY-SITTING

Oguebe was gradually mastering the art of baby-diaper changing. In a situation where he would change the diapers five to six times a day in the interval when Agesi was away at work and Nena was busy in school, the procedure became routine for him.
But there was no way of hastening the apparently simple task of diaper changing.

As Baby Lydia matured she became more active. Up to the age of three months she would lie quietly or make minimal movements while her diapers were being changed. But from age of three months she began to manifest her dislike to certain procedures like applying cold wipes on her. Even when wiper-warmers were employed and the wipes were relatively warm, Baby Lydia sensing the moistness, would instantly realize that it was a wipe and she would not only utter a shrill cry, she would also kick against the disturbance of anyone having to grab her tiny feet while changing her dress.
Often however, the resistance was very momentary once the little lady realized that her removed wet diapers would be replaced with dry warm ones. With time, diaper change became less of a hassle.

Oguebe had never given much thought to the efforts by parents who made possible the nice little dresses worn by the little babies that he saw and often smiled at in church and at the parks. He had never imagined how difficult it might be to change babies' dresses especially after they must have attained the ages of six to nine months and were quite active.

Oguebe then began to understand why most of babies' dresses were made deliberately loose, for ease of passing over their heads.

But even in spite of the designs it could be quite difficult if the baby was cranky, hungry, wet, feeling sleepy or was attracted to something in the vicinity. Passing the dress over the head of the baby often conveyed the impression of asphyxiation and the baby would resist the dress being passed over her head and face. And as the left hand of the baby was passed through, the right hand that was earlier inserted into the dress would be pulled out. Sometimes the same movement would be repeated several times before the baby might feel comfortable and cooperate. Changing Baby Lydia's dress, especially if it was a blouse, was one very difficult aspect of baby-care for Grandpa Oguebe.

Singing or humming of some rhythmic songs while dress-changing would often help sustain the attention of Little Baby Lydia and divert her attention away from resistance. Sometimes, as the baby struggled to ward off the dress, the hand with which she resisted the dress-change would be unwittingly passed into the dress. This good luck was not a regular occurrence. Once in a while as the baby listened to the little rhythmic song and stared Grandpa in the face, her nice little dress was successfully slipped on.

And the leg-stockings too, would be resisted!

As the second pair of the stockings was put on, the earlier pair was often pulled off.

To encounter resistance to some good being done to any individual could be frustrating. But it ceases to appear frustrating when it is remembered that it is a labor of love.

Certainly the enormity of the frustration greatly reduced or completely fizzled away when one realized that the subject who resisted the benevolence was one's granddaughter, a most amiable granddaughter.

As she matured, Baby Lydia appeared to enjoy pulling off her stockings and having them put back in place. She would smile broadly, an enchanting toothless smile, each time she succeeded in pulling off each stocking. She would fling the latter into the air and feel exhilarated on seeing the stocking drop to the ground. It was quite some fun for her, even when the middle-aged amateur baby-sitter was in a hurry to attend to some other things.

Patience was the watch-word when dealing with an adorable and playful *human-puppy*. Any hurry or impatience was out of the question. Attempting to hurry up would only delay matters as a sharp crying protest would ensue from the little princess of the house.

Baby Lydia did not have idea of time.
Who would at her age?
But at all times, she was such a joy to behold.
Grandpa would wish she smiled as often as possible.
But Grandpa would not always stay to play with her.
And leaving her alone with toys even in a secure play-pan, did not always appear to solve the problem.
She treasured the toys for as long as Grandpa was around.
Happily, "Five Little Ducks" children's video almost always pacified Baby Lydia.
But that was not without a pacifier in her mouth!

The little princess would sit glued to watching the little ducks as they jumped into the water in the video. Even when Grandpa knew that getting the little princess hooked on baby-videos from an iPad was not the best thing to do, sometimes he had little option than to oblige her. If only the little lady could be pacified for a while, embattled Grandpa would have some free time.

Would Grandpa recommend the latter to anyone else, grandpas, grandmas or moms? Certainly not!

Would he also recommend routine use of the pacifier for soothing the cranky baby? Certainly not, not even when the individual could readily afford the services of an orthodontist at a later stage. The adolescent granddaughter would not thank Grandpa for the resultant necessary visits to the orthodontist.

The pacifier, that little baby's rubber-molded sucking device, could perform many wonders for crying and fretful babies. It might not be recommended by orthodontists, but it might soon be found to be a sine-qua-non of every household who had babies as young as Little Baby Lydia.

The pacifier soon unwittingly became a second companion for Baby Lydia.

They said pacifiers must be used with caution and not as a habit.

They said it could deform babies' dentition or palate if misused.

Grandpa tried to exercise caution with its use as much as he and the other two players in the house could. But often a choice had to be made between letting Baby Lydia whine without something to pacify her, or, indulging her with a pacifier to suck at when she craved for succor or for comfort.

Yes, the rationalization for a pacifier had to be often deferred even when it was known that protracted use of that little object might adversely affect the configuration of the growing baby's palate or dentition.

Saving the baby's future smile was unfortunately deferred for exigencies of the moment. And the exigency of the moment was to pacify the crying baby.

Which Grandpa would look away when his Little Baby Lydia was crying?

A loving mother would indeed be likely to reach faster for a pacifier when faced with the choice between letting her loved one cry and a possible distortion of the palate.

Little Baby Lydia might get to blame her mom, and not Grandpa, for a distorted dentition.

Certainly, better a little cry now without a pacifier, than a bigger regret with a orthodontist in the future for the convenience of the moment.

Chapter 9

BABY FORMULA OR FORMULA FOR THE BABY

Little Baby Lydia was not a voracious eater. During her first three months she fed very lightly but at very short intervals. She hardly ever spent more than three minutes at a time on the breast. That would be followed by a rest period of a minute or two before the feeding would restart. And she would focus her gaze on her mother as she fed, any time she was being breast-fed. Could she be studying the face of the mother?

Could she be confirming that the mother was happy feeding her?

Could she be wondering whether it was the same person who had fed her the previous day?

Or could she simply be trying to distinguish between the three different faces, grandma, grandpa and mom, whom she had been seeing on a daily basis since her birth?

In any of the cases, it was obvious that Little Baby Lydia was busy studying faces. And the face of the mom who she fed from directly was the one that she bonded with the most.

What bonding in life could be more than that between infant daughter and the mom who was breastfeeding her? The intermittent periods of play with squeezing and scratching of the mother's chin and face was unquestionable evidence of that bond of friendship and love which the infant shared with her mother.

Certainly, human and other-animal psychologists may have a hard time explaining why it is that humans maintain that life-long bonding with their mothers while other mammals who equally breast-feed their young, simply walk away from their mothers on maturity. Could it all be merely part of the consequences of the greater development in humans of the frontal lobe of the cerebrum, as often espoused in mammalian neurophysiology? Human physiologists and psychologists would perhaps enlighten us better.

As she approached six months, Baby Lydia appeared to be a completely different person whenever she was hungry. She would cry so loudly and with such apparent desperation that any on-looker or passer-by would think that she had been starved for a full day or longer. And as she cried, her lips and her tongue would be vibrating simultaneously. And the usually-amiable and adorable face of the little angel would appear cherry-red and angry.
It was better that Little Baby Lydia did not ever cry!
Her cry could make another gentle loving soul wish to cry.
And Nena was once in a while seen to shed some un-intended tears,
Seeing her lovely angel crying right to her face.
And Grandma and even a more stolid Grandpa would plead with broken voices.
They would be asking the angry little bundle of joy to once again smile for their joy.

And when Baby Lydia would finally start smiling again,
Whether she was breast-feeding or bottle-feeding
She would make the process appear all like a fun-party.
She would suck at the breast or the bottle for a short while.

And she would start playing intermittently again to everybody's joy.
If the breast or bottle was mistakenly removed while she played,
The ferocity with which she would grab the food back would suggest an adversary at work.

Baby Lydia appeared more comfortable on the bottle after the first two months.
Perhaps the infrequency of actual breast feeding must have made Baby Lydia to see the bottle rather than the breast as the norm.
In those first two months pumped breast milk as dutifully produced and stored for baby Lydia by her mom Nena, was always available in feeding bottles.
It was all safely stored in the refrigerator for when the need would arise up to twenty-four hours. Nena was informed that if properly refrigerated, that the breast milk could still be used a little longer. But she did not wish to take any chances.
"I would rather discard any unused milk after twelve hours of refrigerated storage. I can always pump more milk for my little baby", Nena said.

Breast milk was the only meal for Baby Lydia for the first three months.
Thereafter, it was occasionally alternated with purchased baby formula as supplement for the little bundle of joy.
The initial introduction of purchased baby formula was often subtly rejected by Baby Lydia.
She would frown her face and remove her lips from the feeding bottle with every initial attempt.
And she would keep her face away from the direction of the bottle for as long as the latter was around her mouth.

Persistent trial and gentle rocking more often than not, did the trick.

If the tip of the teat touched her lips even while she was turning away her face to reject the bottle, Baby Lydia would involuntarily open her lips and welcome the feed.

And she would start sucking again if the teat got thrust into her mouth.

It was so very amazing, how, at such a tender age, the baby recognized which was breast milk and which was baby milk formula. Was it possible that the baby's olfactory organs at that age was so sensitive that she could smell which was mother's milk and distinguish it from cow milk, even from a distance of up to three to four feet away?

But Grandma and Grandpa soon easily learnt a little trick about how to get around the rejection of baby formula.

Whenever pumped breast milk ran short they would gently strive to get the teat that was earlier dipped in a little breast milk and touch the baby's lips. The trick often worked. The baby would open her lips wide. The bottle of baby milk formula would immediately be substituted for mother's breast milk.

And the baby would continue the sucking in earnest. Sometimes, immediately after the swap, the baby would pause a little and appear to want to confirm the authenticity of the milk, before continuing. But with the teat already in her mouth, she would continue the sucking.

The little lady appeared ever so predictable with her every feed.

After the first week of introduction of commercial baby formula, the latter which was initially rejected by Little Baby Lydia, became a preference for her. The fact of the obvious advantages of breast milk and its ready availability was not lost on Nena and her parents. Its psychological advantages on the baby were also well acknowledged. But in view of the baby's preferences and the advantages of storage and transportation, Nena and parents began to combine pumped breast milk with baby formula.

Often the difference between baby formula and pumped breast milk would not be observed by Baby Lydia whenever she was feeling sleepy. But if she was widely awake, she would frown her face at the initial taste of the pumped breast milk which she once preferred.

Initially, Agesi who was usually away from Boston and at work in Western Massachusetts could not believe that a four-month-old Baby Lydia could discern the differences between milk from her mother and the commercial baby formula.

"It is most amazing." Agesi said, as Oguebe narrated the development over the phone to the latter.

It was even more amazing that Baby Lydia could make the differentiation even from a distance and without tasting the milk. As soon as the bottle of breast milk was brought close to her mouth, she would tightly shut her lips or turn her face away. Later she learnt to obstruct the teat of the bottle with her tongue thrust out of her mouth to obstruct the teat!

If the bottle of breast milk was at that stage interchanged with a bottle of baby formula Baby Lydia would open her mouth wide and grab the teat of the feeding bottle containing the baby formula! Amazing! Could her sharp sense of smell discern from a distance the difference between the two types of milk?

Baby formula was relatively expensive. Some brands cost as much as $18 for a tin that would last as little as three days excluding unavoidable waste for a two-month-old baby.
And a tin at four months of age would last even fewer days for Baby Lydia baring waste occasioned by inevitable meal rejections with subsequent discarding. Baby Lydia was maturing fast. And with maturity she was beginning at six months to pick up interest in her surroundings, playing with her toys and keeping herself busy. Her sleeping had also increased in duration, allowing Grandpa to do a few more things during the day. Regular observation of the baby was however seen to be still very essential since Grandpa was always so concerned about possible regurgitation and inhalation of milk. This was more so, since Baby Lydia often fell asleep after most meals.

Nena was making good progress with her studies. She was only four months away from graduation.
Certainly, it had not been easy for any of the three people taking care of Baby Lydia.
Having to travel from Sunderland in western Massachusetts to Boston every Friday and back again to Sunderland on Monday morning had begun to take a toll on Agesi.

On the part of Grandpa, having to stay home all day and to sleep with one eye open at night for Baby Lydia's cry, were not easy to sustain. Having to suspend everything about his private business enterprise, had also begun to take a toll on him.

Having to work extra hard to make up for the nearly one month of lost time of school-work was great stress for Nena. Coming back in the evening to pump breast milk and wake up intermittently at night at the cry of Baby Lydia and again prepare early for school the following morning, both, had also been quite stressful for the latter.

Of the people in the house therefore, it was only Baby Lydia who was not under verifiable stress. To say that she was under no stress at all might be an understatement if not a mis-statement.

Could anyone truly say for sure that young babies felt no stress, simply because they did not voice their feelings except perhaps by crying?

Could anyone say for certain, that the incoherent sounds uttered by babies were not meaningful statements in the baby-world which adults were incapable of discerning?

Could the unavoidable deprivation of a mother's undivided attention at those crucial first weeks and months of existence in an impending tumultuous world, by any stretch of imagination, be classified as "non-stressful" even for a baby?

And could the mere fact of lying in one position on her back and only turning occasionally but in the same bed or cot for not just a day, but for weeks and up to a month or two, not be classified as stress?

Could the fact of not being able to go outside the house on her own except when carried out on a cot, and at the pleasure of an adult, not be classified as stress?

Could the lack of liberty to choose between breast milk and baby milk formula without having to cry for the choice, be truly said not to be a form of stress?

Those were issues which Baby Lydia did not appear physically and mentally equipped to complain about or answer.

But her answers indeed came in form of a shrill cry, to affirm discomfort or a desire for attention. And they came in form of a peaceful sleep or utterance of incoherent sounds, to affirm comfort and satiety with her environment.

Perhaps they were questions which only a babies' advocate or baby science of the future, could answer for her. Perhaps the next generation of child psychologists in concert with next generation of neuroscientists might be able to determine, perhaps with leads on babies' foreheads, what the actual thoughts of babies might be.

But for the moment, Baby Lydia could only express her intents by a shrill cry or by sealing off of her mouth with her tongue at the approach of the teat of a "wrong" feeding bottle.

Yes, even with Grandma and Grandpa sacrificing so much to supplement insufficient parental care, there were many moments in those early days when precise mother's or father's, or both parents' care was necessary if not essential.

But, Baby Lydia could eat, sleep, cry and reject food when she did not feel like eating. Why then would anyone feel that she did not feel those other sensibilities which adults felt?

Baby Lydia could not call anyone by name. She did not participate in the cooking or washing up. She even imposed duties on everyone else in the house.

Did she really impose duties?

No, Little Baby Lydia was not a freeloader.

She gave so much back.

She played an invaluable role in the lives of all that came her way.

She brought more joy to all in the house than any other could do.

She was not a burden.

She was rather a bundle of joy that brightened every face early in the mornings.

When she cried she lit up the house with empathy and humanity.

And when she smiled the radiance tore through any gloom faster than any mood enhancers could ever do. Baby Lydia's steady growth, her sound health and above all her ready radiant smiles were obvious signs of good care jointly ensured by Grandpa and Grandma, even in spite of Nena's tight school schedule.

Grandpa as baby sitter for Baby Lydia and Grandma as Grandpa's Assistant in that arduous duty must have conveyed many more years of healthy living to Baby Lydia than any could readily imagine. The environment was clean and hospitable. And the family love was profound. Those were as opposed to the commercial and group care which Little Baby Lydia might have received at Mama Titi's earlier-contemplated Day Care facility.

As Little Baby Lydia got to three months and started to attempt to hold her neck, Nena was almost in a hurry to get her to start sitting down with supports. Sitting with pillow supports at her back and sides and with outstretched arms made baby Lydia look like a little queen sitting on a little throne.

Yes, she was the little queen of the house and even without uttering a word, she had her orders carried out and promptly too, merely by the semblance of a little cry.

A mere twisting of her face made everyone sit up. But she was a benevolent queen whose often blank countenance left every family member guessing as to what her inner wishes were.

Pillows were initially used to prop up the little lady into a sitting position.
And there she would sit, relaxed and with a blank gaze daring anybody to do anything that would make her cry. And if she as much as appeared to display a sad countenance, everybody in the house would be scrambling to get her to beam a smile if only to light up the surroundings once again.

Soon, after being able to hold the neck steady, Baby Lydia could sit on her own with outstretched hands. Every new week appeared to add a giant leap in her development.

Three month old Baby Lydia relaxing,... upright. (with pillow support)

Chapter 10

THE MOVE TO SUNDERLAND

Time there was when holding of the head was a problem for Baby Lydia.

Time there was when a little wetness elicited instant crying.

Time there was when pillows were lined around "the little lady of the house" so she would have a soft landing on falling forwards or backwards.

But Baby Lydia had matured significantly since leaving Boston for Sunderland. She was taken down to Sunderland to Grandpa and Grandma, so mom could have time to concentrate on the final stages of her studies.

It was a very emotional moment on the Sunday evening when Grandpa and Grandma had to take Baby Lydia on her first journey outside of Boston. Hitherto her only trips outside the house were to the pediatric clinics for checkup or for routine immunization.

But mom needed all the time that she could muster if she must graduate with the rest of her classmates. Already she had lots of outstanding requirements which she needed to complete in the clinics. Those were cases her classmates had already completed. If she did not complete those clinical cases and get successfully signed off for them by her Clinical Attendings, she would not graduate. Even if she scored A+ in all the written exams, she still would not graduate without satisfying the clinical requirements.

And failure to move with her classmates would cost her another six months at the minimum. In addition to the extra time, there might be extra costs in fees. And the fees for each missed or deferred semester ran into several tens of thousands of dollars. There was therefore the need for Nena to do everything possible to graduate on schedule.

The baby's cot, boxes of clothes, feeding materials, feeding bottle warmers, baby's bath-tub and many more paraphernalia than Oguebe had imagined were rolled out in boxes which Nena had spent the previous night packaging. By morning there was hardly any sitting space in the living room.
"I can't really believe that Baby Lydia has gathered so much belongings within just four months of her life", Nena said.
"But you forget that you started gathering these things from the sixth month of pregnancy, Nena", Agesi replied.
"Yes, I remember. But, it is incredible that in just nine months which included about five months before birth, that one tiny little baby has gathered more materials than I have gathered in thirty years!" Nena said.
"It is always that way Nena. After some time, you will find that you will be lacking space for storage of your baby's clothes, toys and other belongings. You will either give out some of these things or you will have to discard some in the garbage otherwise they will overwhelm you." Agesi said.

As mother and daughter discussed her enormous earthly acquisitions, Baby Lydia was sleeping peacefully on the newly-acquired car seat, oblivious of the impending changed environment for her.
Grandpa Oguebe was busy moving the larger items into the trunk of the car.

"I doubt if the car can contain all these things in one trip. The baby's bed and the bassinet have almost taken up all the space. And we have not put in the bags and the numerous boxes. Even if we took up the sitting spaces, we shall still be short of space". Oguebe said.

Standing akimbo and wondering how best to pack the luggage, Oguebe continued:

"I am afraid we may have to leave behind some of the luggage for lack of space. We can collect them during a latter trip to Boston."

"I certainly would want everything to go with you in one trip, Dad, so the baby does not suffer." Nena said. "But we cannot carry things on our laps or on our heads inside the car, can we?"

The discussion about space appeared to be deepening. "A way out is for us to leave out our own bags and concentrate on only baby's things for now. We have enough spares in Sunderland to manage with until we visit Boston again. The other alternative is that Nena can bring our things down piecemeal when she visits." Agesi suggested.

The arrangement worked and all Baby Lydia's belongings were loaded into the car. Even the passengers' seat area in the front was occupied by Baby Lydia's bag of toys.

Nena stood pensively, looking as her father tried to ensure that all Baby Lydia's things were accommodated in the car. After staring at the packing process, she sighed and gently said:

"The passenger's seat in front is taken up by the bag of toys, but I can carry the bag on my laps and go with you guys to Sunderland."

"Go with us to Sunderland?" Oguebe exclaimed in surprise.

"Yes, I can come back by the first bus tomorrow morning for my 10 AM clinic", Nena said.

"But that will be risky, Nena. It will be very uncomfortable for you to carry the bag of toys on your lap. Besides, you may run into problems with traffic police if we happen to be pulled over."

"OK, I will empty the bag and have the toys on the floor mat of the car. I can comfortably have my feet on the toys!"

"If you insist, Nena, but supposing you miss the bus or there is delay on the way tomorrow morning when you are coming back to Boston? That will mean that you will miss your scheduled patient." Agesi said.

"No mom, my first patient is actually by 10.30 AM and the first bus leaves Sunderland by 7.30 AM. It is a two-hour journey. I will have one full hour to play with. I will make it. I wish to spend the first night outside of Boston with Baby Lydia".

"It is not always a two-hour journey, Nena. Sometimes it is a three-hour journey."

"Whatever it is, dad, two hours or three hours, I will make it!"

It was obvious that it would be no use trying to dissuade Nena. It was better to let her travel with Baby Lydia on that first trip out of Boston.

"OK, I will manage the front seat with the toys, Nena, so that you can share the back seat with Baby Lydia in her cot. That way you can stare at her for an extra two to three hours to compensate for the couple of weeks that you may not see her while she is away in Sunderland"

"Great! Mom" Nena exclaimed in excitement.

Nena shared the back seat of the car with Baby Lydia. The latter sat in her car-seat visibly excited at the passing traffic on the Massachusetts Turnpike I-90 West. Her glittering eyeballs dashed sharply from side to side as she appeared to want to see everything that went on around her.

In order not to stress out Baby Lydia on her first long road journey, Grandpa Oguebe decided to stop intermittently at two service plazas along the highway. On each occasion Baby Lydia whose car seat faced backwards was unbelted and brought out of the car. She appeared very alert and appeared to be enjoying the car-ride more than any of the other occupants.

The trip from Boston to Sunderland that ordinarily should take about two hours lasted a little more than three hours because of the stops at the freeway plazas for refreshment.
Finally, Baby Lydia arrived at the home of her grandparents, a modest 4-bedroom two floors house that was to be her home for the foreseeable future.

The unpacking and setting up of the baby's bed and the bassinet lasted some way into the night. A now-tired Baby Lydia slept temporarily on a blanket spread on the floor-carpet in the living room while her bed was being assembled beside Grandma and Grandpa's bed in the master-bedroom.

Nena did not get to spend the night with Baby Lydia by her side as she had planned. The baby's bed needed to be beside Grandma and Grandpa for closer supervision at night. Little Baby Lydia needed to get used to sleeping on her cot in Grandma's bedroom from day one. Besides, Nena needed a good night's sleep so as to get up early to prepare to catch the first bus to Boston.

At least she had satisfied her curiosity of being with her baby on the latter's first night outside of Boston.

Chapter 11

THE LITTLE "PRINCESS OF SUNDERLAND"

An additional occupant had arrived to the "The Little Mansion of Sunderland". The latter was the bombastic name by which Oguebe called his modest four-bed-room single family home situated in a middleclass neighborhood in Sunderland, western Massachusetts. "The little Princess" woke up only once on her first night in her new home. This was as opposed to the average of three times that she used to wake up in Boston, either to feed or to have a change of diapers. She must have been exhausted to a good extent by the unusual journey. But she slept peacefully and only woke up once crying and sucking her fist. None of her pumped breast-milk was transported from Boston to Sunderland. And Nena would not be there in Sunderland to provide pumped breast milk on a daily basis. It was therefore resolved that exclusive baby formula would be commenced from the first night in Sunderland.

Baby Lydia did not appear to feel any differently when she woke up on her first morning in Sunderland. As she woke up a little after 6 AM, she kept turning in her bed and surveyed her surroundings as she was wont to do. She then yawned profusely and, catching a glimpse of a waiting Grandma, she stretched out her arms to the latter with a wide and charming smile. A smile almost always adorned Baby Lydia's face whenever she woke up and saw a familiar face around her. Invariably a cry would have followed if after waking up and surveying her surroundings there was no family member or familiar face around.

A little more than two weeks earlier, the little lady had learnt to smile purposely when happy or comfortable. This was as opposed to the newborn action of her risorius muscles which falsely mimicked a smile largely in the first few weeks of life. She had also learnt to utter some repeated unintelligible sounds which might be mistaken for words.

"Ta, ta, ta" with repeated beating of any nearby toy were Baby Lydia's first babbling words. At five months of age, she was already at the early stages of recognizing objects and babbling in a unique language known only to her.

Grandma and Grandpa felt that their granddaughter was a little ahead of her expected milestones.

By 6.30 AM Nena was ready to leave for the bus-station back to Boston. It was a very emotional first parting from her daughter since the latter's birth. As she muttered "bye-bye" to her daughter, tears streamed down Nena's eyes. But she had to go. She forced herself out of her baby's view towards daddy's waiting car. She then ran back again just as she was about to open the car-door. She came back to repeat the "bye-bye".

Agesi now had to carry Baby Lydia and accompany Nena to the car-garage where a rather impatient Grandpa was repeatedly looking at the car clock.

"Nena remember that if you miss the bus you will miss your patient in the clinic. And that may delay you for six months in the school. Don't provide a good excuse for your being delayed from graduating."

"I know, Dad, it is so difficult for me to leave Baby Lydia."

"But you are not leaving her. You are only traveling for a few days. You will see her in another four days."

"Did you say four days, Dad?"

"Yes, four days. Your mom and I have decided that we will bring Baby Lydia to Boston every weekend until you graduate. That will make it possible for the two of you to see each other every weekend for better bonding."

"That will be great, Dad. Now I can happily travel, knowing that I will see Baby Lydia on Friday."

"Yes, on Friday evening or latest on Saturday morning."

"Is it a promise, Dad?"

"Yes, we promise."

With the assurance that she would see her daughter regularly, Nena briskly entered the car. She shut the door but immediately wound down the glass. Even from a distance Agesi who held out Baby Lydia's little palms in a bye-bye wave could still see Nena's hand as she waved through the car window until the car disappeared from view.

Baby Lydia did not feel any differently. She kept springing up and down in Grandma's hands oblivious of the fact of her first full day outside of the regular morning and evening loving hugs and kisses from her mom.

Back into the house, Agesi had seated Baby Lydia inside her baby's cot. She had put a few toys inside the cot for Baby Lydia to play with while she took a quick shower.

It looked like it would be a good strategy, with some baby's songs ranging from "Five Little Ducks" to "Mama Finger, Mama Finger, Where Are you?" playing melodiously from a baby's computer on a low table nearby.

Agesi had hardly turned on the shower when she heard the loud cry of Baby Lydia from her cot. It started gently but within a few seconds it had developed to full-blown yelling at the top of her voice. Within minutes the usually playful and happy Baby Lydia was crying uninterruptedly like somebody who was being strangulated.

Agesi was alarmed. The crying got so loud and so distressingly pathetic that Agesi thought that maybe Baby Lydia had been trapped somehow between her bed frame and the mattress, or that an insect had stung her. It was akin to the cry of a little child attacked by an invading little animal.

There were no rodents or pets in the house and all the doors were shut.

But still anything was possible.

Baby Lydia had never cried in such a distressing manner before.

Agesi quickly rinsed the soap from her body as much as could rapidly be accomplished. She reached for the bath-towel with which she wiped off the soapy water from her face. She tied the towel round her chest and dashed out of the shower. She nearly slipped but had to grab the towel railing. Like a wounded lioness she ran out of the bathroom to 'rescue' Baby Lydia from whatever it was that was distressing her.

Right there, amidst her many toys and oblivious of everything else sat Baby Lydia. She was not hungry, having been fully fed less than one hour before then. Everything else was intact. There, Baby Lydia sat with her two hands raised up as if in despair and with eyes full of tears. The only thing that was missing at that moment was the company of a most-cherished family member, her mom!

There were no intruding animals; no evidence of insect bite or anything untoward, except for perhaps a fear of abandonment.
Agesi immediately grasped Baby Lydia by both hands and carried her close to her toweled chest.
The yelling immediately stopped but the loud sobs continued for some time. Complete pacification took quite some time and the tears and running of the nose from intensive crying did not quite dry up even up to the time that Oguebe came back to the house from the bus station.
After Grandpa Oguebe had entered the house and shut the door, Baby Lydia kept looking towards the door as if she was still expecting the entry of another person.
Could she be looking for the mom? Could she at such a young age have become conscious of the absence of her mother?

The friendly little smile usually displayed by the little lady when carried shoulder high, was no longer there. She looked neither happy nor sad; just a little apprehensive.

"Could a little baby at that young age recognize the absence of her mother so soon?

Could there have been a sense in her that she had been left inside a cage in a completely strange environment?

Could these have been the impression of this tiny little baby?

Could a mere sudden change of environment have been responsible for this sudden change in mood in Baby Lydia?" Agesi reminisced.

Perhaps the movement to Cumberland should have been done on a Friday evening. Perhaps it should have been done on a Saturday morning so that Nena would stay for up to two full days with Little Baby Lydia in the new environment and gradually withdraw instead of a bye-bye that appeared so sudden, sorrowful and orchestrated.

There certainly was no getting used to baby-sitting or baby-caring; otherwise Agesi and Oguebe would have been experts from their earlier child rearing experience two to three decades previously.

A new life style had started for Oguebe and Agesi. It was to be a strange life-style of second parentage. They had lost the skills about parenting after thirty years since they had their own baby.

But they must have to re-learn the skills for as long as Baby Lydia was around. And the latter was "not going anywhere any time soon" according to Agesi. No, not until Nena graduated.

And even then, Baby Lydia would remain a permanent feature in the lives of the two grandparents, and happily, a joyful feature, to behold and one to be glad about.

Baby Lydia having finally been pacified, Agesi quickly dressed for work and left the house, leaving the care of Baby Lydia in Sunderland solely once again to the lone care of Grandpa, Oguebe.

Grandpa's role as full baby-sitter in Sunderland had finally dawned on him.

What Baby Lydia enjoyed the most was to sit with Grandpa and Grandma together.

She would alternate between climbing up the shoulders of one to climbing up the shoulders of the other. And if her finger nails were not well trimmed, Grandma and Grandpa would need some soothing balms to help with the many razor-sharp scratch marks on their faces and shoulders.

Ever tasted the razor-sharp claws of a young cat?

Little baby Lydia had learnt to study faces.

She would look at grandma and then suddenly switch her gaze to Grandpa.

The intensity of her gaze was so amazing, so piercing.

She could gaze continuously without blinking for minutes on end.

And she made no pretense about who she was gazing at.

What a joy it was to sit at play with Little Baby Lydia after the latter must have been well fed!

But if hungry, sleepy or wet, Baby Lydia would make everybody sit on edge!

Chapter 12

FIRST FULL DAY WITH LITTLE BABY LYDIA IN SUNDERLAND

It did not take long for baby Lydia to again adapt to the environment away from Boston.

All her familiar toys from Boston were still around her. Her usual music from her toys still played the same tunes. Above all, the loving care of Grandpa was still there, full time for her. And Grandma took over where Grandpa left off, always ensuring that the evening baths which Baby Lydia loved so much were always done with water at the right temperature.

Grandma also ensured, among other things, that the little lady's curly African hair was well combed and plaited in lovely little bunches, like little tufts of grass sprouting from a neatly manicured field.

The only thing that changed was that exclusive baby formula replaced a combination of pumped breast milk and baby formula.

Happily, there appeared to be a preference for the taste of baby formula by Baby Lydia. There would have been a big problem if it had been otherwise or if there had been a rejection of baby formula by the adorable little lady in the house.

Baby Lydia did not appear to notice the change in furniture between her Boston environment and her Sunderland environment. There was no way she would be expected to notice, not even with the marked difference between highly urbanized and bustling Boston and relatively rural, docile but exquisitely beautiful Sunderland. Little baby Lydia's little world had not expanded beyond the confines of her cot, the living room and the bedroom. She had not even been allowed into the kitchen and the bathrooms. Her rest room moved around with her, strapped around her waist.

Lady Lydia's bathroom expanded for a mere thirty minutes once in the evenings to a little plastic baby shower tray half-filled with lukewarm water. In the latter little space, the all-demanding little princess would be seated to be bathed once a day in the evenings.

Every other belonging of Baby Lydia's revolved around the living room and her cot in the master bed room. Bits and pieces of baby-stuff littered the living room. Yet it was a rather little world to live in. But it was perfectly sufficient for Little Baby Lydia.

Baby Lydia had plenty of music from her many toys. And the little animals in her baby videos were more than enough movies to entertain her.

"Too much exposure to electronics are not good for babies!" Yes, Grandpa and Grandma knew. But they equally knew that in practice, it was not always possible to resist the temptation of occupying the baby's attention with some interesting kiddies' motion pictures if only to have a little free moment to get certain domestic and other things done while baby was awake.

And so, Baby Lydia found all the love, all the care and all the fun in her little enclave in Sunderland. Her world only loomed larger when she was later to be taken to the gazebo section of the house to look at the rear gardens. She was further, to her great excitement, taken to the front of the house to have a good view of the lawns, the many trees and a few passing cars.

As she gazed in silence, she clutched tenaciously at Grandpa's shirt as she apparently marveled at the larger world of woods and gardens, a scenario which she might have been missing in the Boston Apartment.

There was no way of ascertaining which location was preferable for Baby Lydia, Boston or Sunderland. But certainly, given that mom was domiciled in Boston, Baby Lydia certainly would have preferred Boston to Sunderland. Nothing could be compared to mom's tender loving care for a fragile little baby, not even the combined loving care of Grandpa and Grandma. How lucky then for any who had all three sources of affection combined in those tender early months.

A daddy's added love would have made the circle complete and unsurpassable. But where the latter was a thousand and more miles away, the nearest best thing to completeness would suffice, especially since nobody missed greatly, what he or she had not tasted.

At exactly five months and six days Baby Lydia had become able to crawl but only on her belly. Hitherto she would simply purposely fall forwards from the sitting position and remain sprawled on the floor looking up for help. This was shortly after she moved to Sunderland.

At first if a toy was placed close to her and the toy lay outside her reach, she would stretch her hands and often start beckoning on the toy with her fingers as if commanding the toys to come closer.

After repeated failed attempts to reach the desired object from the sitting position, she would try to stretch and kick her legs. Sometimes the kicking would push the toy further away from her. She would then stretch herself forward until she would inadvertently fall forward on her belly. Thereafter by rhythmic kicking backwards and stretching of her hands and clutching at anything close by, she would succeed in pulling herself forward towards the desired toy. The practicing was started in Boston where the wooden floor of the living room did not quite provide enough frictional resistance that would thrust her forward to reach the desired toy. The movement forward on her belly was much easier in Sunderland with the aid of the carpeted floor.

On the evening of the first day in Sunderland Oguebe had placed Baby Lydia on the carpeted floor of the living room with some toys around her. It did not take long before Baby Lydia flattened herself on her belly and restarted her practice of dragging herself forwards on her belly. The increased frictional force provided by the floor-carpet easily thrust the baby forward with each kick. It was so dramatic! And Baby Lydia appeared to relish the moment. She repeated the movement again and again. She was excited as she grabbed the toy which hitherto had been outside of her reach.

Once she succeeded with reaching the toy of her desire by crawling on her belly, there was no going back for Baby Lydia. Thereafter for the rest of the day, Baby Lydia would go flat on her belly immediately she was sat down.

A new day had dawned for the baby in the house on the first full day in Sunderland.

What a difference a single day in a new environment could make.

Baby Lydia had started belly-crawling!

She had been seen falling forwards on her tommy a day or two earlier in Boston. On each occasion she lay there kicking her legs backwards and making funny noises, halfway crying, halfway smiling. Everybody thought it was an accident or simply a mistaken fall from the sitting position.

But on that first full day in Sunderland, the little Baby of the House had learnt to propel herself forward!

Holding her neck and being able to sit upright were major milestones in Baby Lydia's development. But being able to move on her own from one spot to another was in itself a very major milestone.

It meant that one could no longer sit the little baby on one spot and move into the bathroom and hope that she would still remain in that position one minute after being left on her own.

It meant that objects that should not be reached or handled by the baby must be removed from the floor and kept out of reach. Above all, it meant that all dangling electrical wires must be safe-guarded. It further meant that electrical sockets that were accessible from the floor must be temporarily sealed off.

The impact of the presence of an additional tenant in Sunderland had begun to be felt. And for as long as Little Baby Lydia was around, things in the house would never remain the same again.

As Baby Lydia thrust herself forwards, her attention was very often towards any books around her. Even when toys were placed around her, she would reach out for the nearest book in sight. It was amazing how she always knew which was the book among the many toys.

Luckily there were thick-page baby's books among her toys.

Baby Lydia loved books, especially brightly-colored ones.

She also loved photos of books in computers. But she would often fumble at, and sit on top of the electronic books. She would admire and endlessly attempt to grab the images and the A, B, C, D drawn on electronic books.

"A is for Apple, B is for Bus, C is for Cat, D is for Dog". As these letters were rattled and the images of the relevant objects displayed, a fascinated Baby Lydia would listen for a few seconds with apparent rapt attention. But the listening and attention would be for only a few seconds! Thereafter an apparently-agitated Baby Lydia would spring forward to grab the object that was being displayed. It would become a struggle. Even with Grandpa acting as a devoted teacher the little student would kick at, rather than read the books.

"Little Baby Lydia enjoyed tearing books. where she could not tear them, as in electronic books, she would kick at them"

Chapter 13

LITTLE BABY LYDIA TRAPPED

Baby Lydia was on the move as soon as she mastered the art of moving herself from one spot to another. There was no going back!

Like they did with the head-holding and sitting upright milestones, Grandma and Grandpa took copious photos and videos of baby Lydia as she laboriously thrust herself forward on her belly in the following few days.

As Baby Lydia became mobile on her belly, new challenges crept up. Over the course of the following four days, the belly crawling got perfected.

A new problem arose about how to guard Baby Lydia from crawling on her belly up to the staircase which was contiguous to the second floor living room. If she crawled up to the open staircase, Baby Lydia might be tempted to want to get down the staircase and that would be disastrous. The likelihood of such a scenario was remote considering that the speed of the belly-crawling was still very slow. But at the speed of development of new "tricks" by Baby Lydia, such a scenario could not be ruled out especially if Grandpa or Grandma was on the computer and got distracted from the crawling little lady for any length of time.

The idea of use of pillows as barricades then cropped up.

"Why don't we barricade the area around Baby Lydia with pillows. She has not learnt how to push away objects on her path." Agesi suggested

Pillows were thus placed some distance around the baby to allow her space to crawl but at the same time to limit the space within which she would operate. It was believed that Baby Lydia was not yet articulate enough to clear obstacles from her path. Yes, such maneuver was considered to be too articulate for her at that stage.

The idea of using pillows as barricades worked but only for some three weeks.
By the fourth week of her learning to belly-crawl, a disaster nearly occurred.
Grandma had as usual left early for work. Grandpa who had literary relocated his private home office to the dining room, was busy on a computer. Many of Grandpa's files and working materials were already almost permanently stationed on the dining table which overlooked the living room. From his temporary office chair in the dining room Grandpa could therefore directly see what was happening in the living room. His eyes darted intermittently between the computer screen and the little lady who was belly-crawling around in the living room.
Grandpa must have steadied his gaze on the computer screen for a little too long.
He had momentarily forgotten that there abounded in the room, a little young lady who needed to be observed every now and then. And the little young lady, even when she could not walk, could reach unwanted places crawling on her belly. And she would do so noiselessly. And she was so tiny that she could creep into tiny little spaces between barricades and between furniture.
And within a minute or two of Grandpa's looking away, the young lady had disappeared from the radar.

A loud and shrill scream that emanated from the far end of the spacious living room instantly broke Grandpa's attention from the computer screen!

Baby Lydia had surprisingly crawled behind the sofa at the far end of the living room. She had crawled under the linen flap that covered the back of the sofa and was crying shrilly from within the space at the back of the large sofa.

Grandpa had sprung to his feet at the first shrill cry of Baby Lydia and had hoped to see the baby still on the carpet in the living room. But Baby Lydia was not seen. Only the shrill cry emulating a baby in distress was heard. Grandpa quickly peered behind the sofa in the direction of the baby's cry but Baby Lydia was not seen.

In a flash, the now vividly-frightened Grandpa cleared the furniture-obstacles and made his way behind the sofa and in a frenzy, raised the flap that covered the back of the sofa.

And there on the floor lying on her belly with outstretched hands lay Little Baby Lydia. Her two outstretched hands were glued to a black plastic tray of mouse glue trap which Grandpa had long forgotten. The little lady was vigorously struggling to free herself from the glue trap. But in the process of struggling to free herself, she was trapping herself the more. Her face was only an inch or two away from the very adhesive glue trap. If she had pulled herself a little further forward, her face too would have been trapped. And if her lips were caught by the glue, she might not be able to utter a cry! A trap that had been set for mice had caught an adorable little princess in her home!

Many months earlier, Grandpa and Grandma had seen some six to ten black solid particles the sizes of sunflower seeds behind the microwave oven in their kitchen. Certainly, if the particles were brownish or coffee-colored they would have been mistaken for sunflower seeds or flaxseeds. But they were black in color and were in a hidden corner, the sort of place that rodents would like to visit at night. Agesi who first saw the "black seeds" immediately called Oguebe who confirmed that the supposed "seeds" were indeed rodent droppings.

"Rodent droppings behind my microwave? How are we sure that there may not be some also within the microwave itself? And where could the rats have entered from?" Agesi exclaimed.

Even when they had not physically seen any rats or mice in the house, the couple had been very worried about the possibility of having rats inside their living room.

"Rats' poop in our living room?" Agesi had exclaimed on that occasion.

Consequently, Grandma and Grandpa had proceeded to purchase all kinds of mouse traps ranging from glue traps to small metallic mouse traps which they littered in all possible hiding spaces for any rats in the house. They had dreaded any thought of leptospirosis, the deadly disease that was transmitted through urine of rats and some other animals.

"It is not impossible that rats could find their way into our house especially through the car garage which is often left open for long periods of time." Agesi said.

They remembered that they had seen a mouse run out of the car garage on the day that they came to inspect the house for purchase many years earlier. That singular incidence almost made them to withdraw their bid for the house. But the home owner had assured them that the incidence that they witnessed was atypical and that there were no rats in the premises.

The sight of the sun-flower seed-sized pellets near their microwave oven again aroused the couple's fears that there might indeed be rodents lurking around the house.
The need therefore arose for littering every suspicious hidden space with all kinds of mouse traps including glue traps.

One of such abodes for rodents' traps was the hidden space under the sofas in the living rooms. Little did grandpa or Grandma ever imagine that a crawling little Baby Lydia would ever find her way to the underside of the sofa. None imagined that the little space behind the sofa would be her favorite spot to visit! They did not imagine that a baby that young, could lift the flap behind the sofa and crawl into the little space within the three-seater sofa to get glue-trapped! As of the time of purchase and dispersal of the glue and other traps, there was no plan of bringing Little Baby Lydia to Sunderland. Indeed, the little lady had not even come into the world.
And when the house was being prepared for the relocation of the little princess from Boston to Sunderland, nobody thought of mouse traps which in any case were well hidden from view of ordinary residents and visitors. But Little Baby Lydia was no ordinary resident or visitor.

Ordinary residents and visitors did not crawl on their bellies. And they did not go seeking obscure little spaces for any reason.

Now, there, was Little Baby Lydia with her two tiny palms simultaneously glued firmly unto the tray of tenacious black glue stationed in place to trap rats! The little baby had pulled aside one of the pillows that barricaded her and had crawled a distance of nearly ten feet to the far end of the living room. One of her little toys was seen sticking out from the rear side of the sofa. She must have been pushing it forward as she belly-crawled forward until the toy got behind the flap at the back of the sofa.

Baby Lydia was apparently attempting to retrieve her toy from under the sofa. She must have tried several maneuvers before succeeding to angulate her head sideways to get it into the little space behind the flap at the back of the sofa. It was a frightful sight.

As Grandpa jumped to his feet he inadvertently pulled the charging cord of the computer off the machine which came crashing down as Grandpa ran up to the baby.

Grandpa grabbed the baby by the shoulders with one hand while trying to hold the back flap of the triple-seater with the other hand. The space through where Baby Lydia entered into the back of the sofa was so small that it was inconceivable how she managed to angulate herself into the tiny space

A very quick decision needed to be made on which to pay more attention to: lifting the flap of the sofa for a clearer view of the inside of the sofa, or freeing the hands of the baby from the glue trap while she was still trapped inside the sofa.

Grandpa who had become almost hysterical had to drop back Baby Lydia and pull up the sofa with both hands so as to clear it completely from the baby. Only thus was Baby Lydia placed in full view to be rescued from her obviously-trapped position inside the sofa. Grandpa thereafter tried to retrieve Baby Lydia's hands from the glue but the tenacity appeared to hurt the baby. She cried the more at every little attempt. Grandpa therefore lifted up Little Baby Lydia out of the enclosed space in the sofa. This was done along with the two plastic trays of glue onto which the baby's tiny fingers were glued. The tray of glue dangled along as the baby was pulled out of the sofa.
With the baby, the tray of glue and all manner of debris which had been accumulating unnoticed under the sofa and now tenaciously stuck to the glue as the retrieval of the baby was going on, Grandpa Oguebe made a dash to the bathroom.

As the victim of the entrapment still cried and struggled to free her hands, she entangled her dress and Grandpa's shirt into the glue. It became an increasingly messy situation as Grandpa had to struggle to ensure that the baby as she kicked her feet vigorously in protest, did not also entrap her feet or her trunk.
The baby, Grandpa's shirt, debris and the all-entrapping glue had to be meticulously lowered into the shower tray with the tenacious glue complicating an already bad situation.
More hands would have been needed to steady the struggling baby as Grandpa made a dash to the bathroom drawer to obtain cotton buds and some diluted spirit.
Application of mere soap and water was of little help.

A cotton bud dipped in a drop of spirit came to the rescue when applied on the trapped palms and fingers. These were rinsed copiously with running water. The entrapped fingers were freed even when the stickiness remained with matted debris on the individual fingers. The job of dislodging the glued clothing material was a job for a later moment.

No one would have believed that Little Baby Lydia could belly-crawl that far. No one would have believed that she would be able to pull aside the barricading pillows on her way!!!
And how did she learn to angulate her head to the side to be able to get into that little space behind the sofa?
Could crawling little babies be that much more capable than most adults could imagine?
Agesi soon called from work midday as she was wont to do. When she spoke with Oguebe, she found it difficult to believe that the baby who the previous two to three weeks could only sit at a spot and beckon on objects, was able to crawl ten feet and stick her head beneath a sofa.
"Thank God it was not a metallic trap!" were the first words that emanated from Agesi when she was informed over the phone of the little domestic accident involving Baby Lydia and the glue traps.
"It is chilling to imagine what would have happened to our little baby's fingers if we had used metallic mouse traps in the rooms instead of only in the ceilings." Agesi further said.
After that event, all mouse traps in Agesi and Oguebe's household found themselves inside the trash cans.
Mouse traps that had never caught any mouse had had their first victim; a most improbable victim: Little Baby Lydia.

Oguebe loved recording images and taking photos of funny and unusual situations. But that glue trap incidence on the first full day in Sunderland was far too serious a scene to be recorded. It was an obvious domestic emergency far too serious and dangerous to give time for recording. There was even no time whatsoever for any thoughts about recording the emergency.

It was a serious call to action in arranging safer and stronger barricades to protect Baby Lydia from physical harm consequent upon her new milestone of crawling. That was even when it was still more of body-dragging on her belly rather than actual crawling!

It became more glaring that even when the spaces between the furniture were barricaded with bags and boxes, that Little Baby Lydia would always find a way to push aside the barricades and create playgrounds behind the furniture.

A new lesson was thus taught to Grandpa and Grandma

It was indeed a lesson for all baby-sitters and those who engage their noble services.

It is a call for better appreciation of what should be a most priced profession but which is hardly ever recognized as a profession.

It is a call for society's re-evaluation of all that go by the name of baby-sitters:

that crop of angels whose value is often underestimated and invariably underpaid.

Baby-sitters belong to that crop of men and mostly women whose crucial jobs are neither taught in high schools nor in colleges, but upon whose shoulders the young offspring of some rich and famous who shun institutionalized day-care or who cannot secure places in same, rest for succor.

It is a call for better appreciation of the tribe of invaluable "jobbers" whose all-important services are often denigrated or consigned to undocumented immigrants or the dredges of itinerant job market.

It is a call for inclusion into the school or college curriculum of an all-important subject which caters for society's young and vulnerable especially in the face of increasing involvement of both parents in full time employments.

Day-care centers do great jobs.

But the question remains: would society benefit or be worse off by formally inculcating "Baby-sitting" as a course of its own in our higher institutions?

By so doing, Grandpa, Grandma, Student moms and amateur baby-sitters could take on formal or informal courses of study for greater efficiency and better safety.

Thus, Oguebe, Agesi, and indeed Mama Titi, would refresh their experiences, ensure better sanitary conditions, and glue traps in obscure places would not be forgotten before a Baby Lydia is brought down to reside in Grandpa and Grandma's home in Sunderland.

Thus, will baby-sitters of the future claim their rightful places in a society that has for long neglected and underestimated them.

Little Baby Lydia
Loved crawling between
narrow spaces and barricades
and she occasionally got trapped in
between furniture and barricades put in-
place to checkmate her.

Chapter 14

RAPID DEVELOPMENT OF NEW MILESTONES

The following few days in Sunderland saw Baby Lydia
making giant strides in development.
Belly crawling was very transient. By the third week of
crawling on her belly, the little lady learnt that she
progressed faster by steadying one knee on the carpet
and pulling forward the alternate knee and hence
propelling her body forward. It was so fascinating how
every little new movement had to be practiced again
and again and perfected upon, before advancement to
the next movement.
With Baby Lydia being able to crawl on her knees, the
entire second floor of the house became her empire.
Increasing challenges for effective care cropped up.
Not only were pillows no longer an obstacle, they
indeed became a little risky because she would grab
any pillow on her path and stick her face on it as if
trying to experiment on self-suffocation. And as she
stuck the pillow on her face and struggled with it, she
would hold the pillow tighter against her face while
she struggled against it. It often appeared like a cat's
play but it called for concern and was often frightful to
any adult onlooker.
Baby Lydia's care had begun to assume new
dimensions as she developed new ideas.

The greatest challenges became the staircase, electrical wires and electric power sockets. The little lady always appeared attracted to those unwanted areas. And she always got very fascinated with attempting to pull out cords from wall-sockets.

It was relatively easier to block the staircase with bags stacked on top of one another. Luckily Baby Lydia never attempted to climb the bags on the stairway. But there was no guarantee that she would not experiment with them one day, just as she did with making her way behind the sofa into the glue trap.

Blocking the entrance and exit to and from the staircase created problems for the adult resident and for any visitors. The job of having to clear big bags from the staircase each time one wanted to go downstairs was not much fun. But it was a burden that needed to be borne, until the idea of installing a professionally-designed baby barrier was suggested by a visiting friend who had gone through the job of raising a toddler herself. Before the installation of the staircase gate, the second floor living room looked like a hoarder's abode with all kinds of bags retrieved from various rooms and stacked haphazardly on top of one another within view of homeowners and visitors alike.

The idea of flower vases and low-hanging picture-frames had to be discarded. Any of those could constitute dangerous weapons for a literally-rampaging crawling little lady.

Yet it was fun to behold!

It was great fun watching a busy little human being living in a world of toys, stacked bags and thick-cover story books which the little lady could not yet read or even appreciate, but which she relentlessly fumbled with.

It was even more fun listening to the little lady chuckling to herself and to the toys in a language which she alone appeared to understand.
Nothing could be more fascinating than seeing a world of little worries or indeed no worries whatsoever.
A world of complete contentment often thought impossible was daily manifesting before the eyes of Grandpa and Grandma as they watched Baby Lydia grasp and bang her toys with full attention and concentration. Such attention and concentration would be near impossible for any adult to manifest.

The stair-case gate that was initially purchased could not fit because it was obstructed by the big brass-handrailing on the staircase. It was either the handrail would be dislodged or the purchased stair-case gate was returned. The former option would deform the house while the latter option of abandoning the idea was not tenable in view of Baby Lydia's new adventurism.
It was later decided to purchase and install a shorter staircase gate which would not be obstructed by the handrail on the gate.
The installed device turned out to fit quite effectively especially as it did not involve boring holes on the walls.
Baby Lydia was initially afraid of the beautiful white gate. She appeared suspicious of it.
She would crawl close to it and then stop some distance short, and stare at it for a while.

She would then utter some unintelligible words as if she was asking some questions from the white new object. She would thereafter make a U-turn and crawl back to the center of the living room. For two days the new gate kept the little lady away from the staircase. By the third day however after she appeared to have gotten used to seeing the gate, Baby Lydia, on getting close to it, crawled very rapidly past the gate. She would then turn around to stare in amazement at the gate before crawling briskly to the farther side of the corridor.

Before the expiration of one week, the seven-day wonder about the gate was over. It looked like the fast-maturing lady had made friends with the newly-installed white structure between the corridor and the staircase.
Baby Lydia appeared to muster more courage and crawled up to the staircase gate and stopping a little short of touching the latter. She peeped down the staircase through the spaces between the railings on the gate. She did not at first attempt to push or pull against the gate as she always did on chairs. She appeared a little afraid of the gate's railings and the flight of stairs. She briefly peeped at the stairs through the bars on the gate and quickly crawled away.
The gate thus appeared to have fulfilled the purpose for which it was installed. And that was to keep Baby Lydia away from the staircase.

Everything appeared to be falling perfectly into place. However, it looked like when one problem was over, another had readily popped up. Baby Lydia would stealthily crawl into the kitchen while Grandma or Grandpa was cooking or pouring out hot water from the kettle. And she would pull on the clothing of the individual who might not be aware of her presence. The first time she did it, she dislodged the kettle of hot water from Grandpa's hand. But luckily the hot water which missed the mouth of the Thermos flask, spilled on the cooker. The hot water narrowly missed the face of Baby Lydia who, while pulling on Grandpa's dress, was looking upwards on Grandpa.

A second gate had to be installed to barricade the kitchen from the corridor.

Still, the problems were not over with yet. The dining room was directly open into the living room. And the space was too wide to be covered by even the widest extended gate in the stores.

The boxes which were earlier discarded from the staircase were therefore pulled back into play. Every available bag and paper-box in the house was rolled out to the living room to help cover the wide space between the dining room and the living room.

The defacing aesthetics were readily preferable to any domestic accidents. Indeed, at that stage, nobody was thinking of aesthetics any longer.

The house was beginning to look like a mass of barricades. But it did not matter. All aesthetics must submit to Little Baby Lydia's safety.

A bundle of joy was there in little Baby Lydia to dispel any and all other burdensome thoughts.

Chapter 15

BABY LYDIA GOES TO THE DINER

To celebrate the relocation of Baby Lydia to Sunderland, Agesi and Oguebe took the little family to a diner. It was not Baby Lydia's first entry into an eatery. She had visited a couple of fast food locations in company of her mom and grandparents in Boston including McDonalds, Burger King, and a number of others. But it was her first formal visit with her family since she started being more aware of solid foods. She had indeed started showing signs of recognition of the smell of delicious foods.

As soon as Grandpa and Grandma sat down and the appetizers were served, visible agitation to get out of the cot was noticed from Baby Lydia's end. She started kicking and crying with her hands continuously raised in the direction of the food.

"I want the cookies, not the cot!", appeared to be her unexpressed plea.

The little lady obviously had matured more than Grandma, Grandpa and Mom, could imagine.

The crying immediately ceased as soon as the little lady was unstrapped from the cot and placed on a high chair which nobody had imagined she would be able to sit comfortably on, as yet.

As the adults settled down to savor the desserts Little Baby Lydia was visibly salivating and stretching out her hands in the direction of the food. There was initial hesitancy about giving adult food to Baby Lydia in a commercial diner. But as the little lady kicked and protested, Mom, decided to try a little bit of the sauce on the tongue of the little lady. The baby gulped the paste after initially squeezing her face as if in rejection. Thereafter a little more of the mashed potatoes was tried and then a little mashed beef. And the little lady felt she was as of right a comfortable part of the party. She was soon making the repeated unintelligible sentences which she usually made when she was happy.

It was such great joy to Nena, seeing her little girl who was just about one, sitting comfortably at diner with the rest of the family and enjoying some of the dishes that were being served.
She tried to see everything that was being done.
She would love to clutch at every dish that was being served, even when cautiously restrained by her mother.
Even before the dish was placed on the table she spread out her hands to catch the plate.
Nice words and compliments from the waiters and waitresses did not satisfy her desires.

Each of three adult family members was seeking to feed her in the diner.
Each would feel honored to have her accept a morsel from him or her. It was ensured that spices were strictly kept away from the menu.
And if the little lady dipped her fingers into any dish, the owner would smile and thank her for the approval.

Who, could wield so much subtle authority, but Little Baby Lydia?
Who could command so much attention?
Even Rider Haggard's "She Who Must Be Obeyed" was not so powerful and yet so humble.
Three doctors babysitting you in turns!
And each felt it as both a privilege and a duty!
And each felt so fulfilled sitting and playing with you!
They would roll on the carpet as you rolled.
They would giggle as you giggled.
And they felt young again every minute of staying with you.
And the ticking of the clock appeared to hasten.
And they followed your belly-crawling, your knee-crawling and your unsteady gaits
And every staggering step rebounded with joy when you started to run
And the wide gait and staggered steps were so much fun to observe.

And if dad was around, the circle would have become complete.
But the love of Mom, Grandma and Grandpa were boundless and tried to compensate.
And your uncles, aunts and multiple admirers poured in more affection than any could wish for.
And your every wish was their command.
If you cried they sprang to their feet.
And if you smiled, you made their day.

When you were awake they kept an eye.
And when you slept they also kept an eye.
Even when you ferociously fought against sleep as you often did,
they cuddled you to their chests and still kept an eye.
And they wished you would readily lose the fight against sleep.

And when you surrendered and slept, mom would still
keep an eye.
What a beautiful thing to be a little baby!
And not just to be a baby, but to be Little Baby Lydia.

How many men and women know
By failure to participate in the life-renewing gift of
babysitting grandchildren,
What they lose in peace of mind and self fulfilment
What they miss in every smile and in every babble?
How many indeed know or remotely appreciate
What priceless joy and infinite renewal that they miss?
How many indeed will ever appreciate
What jewel of inestimable value that passes them by?
How many, forever will never come to appreciate
the joy and fulfilment which their own Baby Lydias
held in stock for them?

There is a Little Baby Lydia out there for everyone
Yes, there is one for everyone, biological or non-
biological, it really matters not.
And no amount of earthly treasures, diamond or gold
No amount of fame, private jets, brick and mortar,
can substitute for a Baby Lydia in our, or indeed in
any other lives.

And while diamond and gold can be chanced upon,
Or by sheer hard work, by innovation, by lottery or
cheating, be acquired
The inanimate pieces of metal grossly treasured by
man,
Can bring fleeting smiles on faces of the fool and the
wise alike.
But no matter how much the latter are treasured
They can never smile back or present palpable breath
of life.

They can never utter the lovely toothless smile of a
Little Baby Lydia.

Who but a nigh-fairly princess would bring such joy?
You made heads turn in admiration wherever you
went.
And the encomiums were not mere formalities, but
were all from the heart.
The spontaneous expression "Lovely Baby" emanated
from every lip,
in your pram, at the shops and even in elevators.
And if you happened to beam a smile, the joy would
be complete
And your black curly hair when plaited in bunches,
Accumulated encomiums from all and sundry
And they made the day for all that you came across.

You make the experience of being a grandparent come
really home.
And grandpas and grandmas everywhere will draw
inspiration from your story.
And they will thank you for making vacillating student-
moms to take a stand.
They will find courage to plan well and have their
babies when they so desired
And not defer forever a decision that would confer life-
long joy and fulfilment
And the world will be the happier for concerned
grandpas and grandmas
And "Little Baby Lydia" will be on their every lip.

Chapter 16

BABY LYDIA GOES TO CHURCH

Little Baby Lydia had turned eight months. She was maturing steadily by the day.

Cereals had begun to be added into her milk from her fifth month. It was noticed that baby formula alone was no longer enough for her. She was not a voracious feeder. But being very active she readily burnt out energy and did not appear to be gaining weight. She was however in ninety-five percentiles in height but only forty-five percentiles in weight. It was recommended that mashed potatoes, mashed vegetable like carrots, peas and mangoes be added to her diet.

But Baby Lydia would only taste those delicacies once or twice and squeeze her face. She would thereafter sharply turn away her face at the approach of the plastic spoon. If her head was forcefully steadied she would tighten her lips or obstruct entry of the spoon into her mouth with her tongue. She was always so decided on what she wanted and what she did not want, even from those early stages of life. Persistence in feeding her against her will would result in violent kicking of her legs and twisting away her frame in the opposite direction. If at that stage she was obliged and left on the floor, she would very briskly crawl away as fast as she could.

Baby Lydia had ben to Sunday Church services several times with her mom and grandparents. But she had not been formally admitted as a Christian by Baptism according to the religious beliefs of her parents and grandparents.

She needed to be baptized in the church to be a fully-admitted member of the Church of her parents' Christian denomination.

The local Catholic Church where her family members worshipped, on request, had set up a date for her Baptism. Agesi and Nena went for shopping for her Baptism dress. Oguebe accompanied them to the shopping Mall.

Oguebe had thought that it was a straight-forward process of entering the shop and choosing the baby's size of Baptismal dress. It turned out to be a very detailed multiple store search from Burlington to Macey's; from Target to Michaels to Walmart and back to Burlington.

Grandpa was getting impatient if not worn out.

Surprisingly Baby Lydia did not appear worn out as she stayed awake throughout the search period to and from the Mall to Walmart. She only bottle-fed intermittently and playing with her pacifier and toys in the stroller.

At last a matching crystal white Baptismal dress with matching headband was purchased from Burlington after a third visit.

Baby Lydia looked like a little fairy queen, more like the paintings of imaginary winged Angels seen on the walls in churches.

It was decided that photographs of her in her Baptismal try-on dresses be not taken until the actual Baptism day which was the following day.

True to expectation the Baptism girl was a beauty to behold in her beautiful all-white dress with white stockings and white head ribbons and bands.

She behaved so well during the event. Even when "Baptismal Holy Water" was poured on her forehead in conformity with traditional Baptismal rituals, the sturdy Baby Lydia did not cry as many babies were wont to do. She stared steadily at everybody and even stretched out her hands to be carried by the officiating Minister. She was so friendly at Baptism. Her God-parents as well as her mother and grandparents surrounded her at the altar. Her uncles had also traveled long distances to attend the christening ceremony. She officially took the name of Lydia, a name which Nena and Dave had given to her well in advance of her birth.

A middle name of Theresa was also given even though Lydia as her known name had fully stuck as her only name.

Although Lydia was her name, hardly anybody called her simply by that name. Little Baby Lydia was the name by which everybody knew her.

Family members and family friends were received after her Baptism in Baby Lydia's living-room abode in the family home in Sunderland.

The many ungainly bags which served as barricades against Baby Lydia crawling astray had been temporarily removed for aesthetic reasons and to accommodate the guests.

With so many people in the living room, Baby Lydia found so much company that she initially appeared overwhelmed by the presence of so many strange faces. However, she soon adapted to the crowd and was crawling all over the living room.

Two of the guests also came with babies and so there was good company later on the first floor living room for Baby Lydia and her young guests.

Baby Lydia loved people. She was very excited to see other babies around her for the first time. It was so amazing how she was able to recognize that those were people and not merely big toys which she occasionally had around her.

Two adults took turns to supervise the young celebrant and her two young guests of about the same eight to twelve-month age group.

Baby Lydia was very sociable. She loved company of other babies.

Little Baby Lydia learning to play with cousins and other friends

Chapter 17

BOSTON REVISTED; SAVORING THE HARBOR-POINT

As Nena's graduation approached, her schedule appeared more hectic and almost more desperate. "Many of the patients booked for observation or clerking by the medical students do not turn up on schedule" Nena complained.
"There are so many no shows. This may be because most of the patients that we see are on one form of assistance or another and do not pay a penalty for canceling without notice. Many of them do not appear to treasure the attention that they receive."
Nena complained.
"It is not unusual Nena, but you just have to persevere. To succeed in this profession, you just have to be patient and empathetic. Some of the patients are troubled in other ways. Therefore, when they are delinquent or default in certain ways, one needs to be a little more understanding with them." Agesi advised.

It was obvious that there were lots of frustrations on the paths of the medical and dental students as regards their satisfying their clinical requirements. Invariably however, at the end of the day, all the students who had been able to make it to the final year ended up satisfying their requirements with varying degrees of success. They might not all be honors graduates but most of them being very bright students, would eventually succeed and obtain their degrees.

Agesi and Oguebe had not quite kept up with their earlier pledge to take Little Baby Lydia to Boston every Friday. They did it once or twice and the stress and hassles were too much. It was so much burden to load in and off-load all the paraphernalia associated with the baby every Sunday evening from Boston to Sunderland and then back again from Sunderland to Boston every Friday evening.

After running the routine for two consecutive weeks, which translated to eight loading and off-loading runs, the couple were weary of the frequent movement.

"My back will break if I continue in this way, Agesi. We are not getting any younger. We have to limit these loading and off-loading of baby stuff in and out of the trunk. Besides, the to-and-fro from Boston to Sunderland is already telling on my waist. We must soft-pedal." Oguebe complained.

"You made the promise to Nena, O.G, but it is up to you to fulfil or to break it. But I don't even think that it will help her studies for us to keep disturbing her with visits every week when other students are busy concentrating on their studies."

"So, should we stop visiting?"

"No, not necessarily?"

"What then, do you suggest?"

"We should visit every other weekend. That way we rest adequately for one weekend before we set out on the following weekend."

"OK, sounds good!"

Thus, was the earlier promise of scheduled weekly visits to Boston broken, at least temporarily.

Nena's tone during her phone conversations with Oguebe and Agesi that weekend portrayed deepening loneliness and eagerness to see her baby more regularly.

"I long every day, to see Baby Lydia" She told Agesi in a rather hoarse voice.

"I dream every night about her", she further said.

Agesi was very much moved by Nena's pleas. She remembered vividly when Nena herself was a baby. She remembered how much she always wanted to be by little Nena's side.

"Never mind Nena we will bring Baby Lydia to Boston every weekend hereafter until you graduate."

"But, have you discussed with daddy?"

"No, not on these renewed weekly visits. But I will talk to him."

"Another promise, Mom. Will this one be fulfilled?"

Yes, this new promise needed to be fulfilled because Agesi and Oguebe themselves would want a day of freedom from baby-sitting at least once every week. And Oguebe had started complaining of feeling imprisoned in the house from 7.30AM every day until 5.30PM when Agesi would be back from the clinic. His home office was taking a big hit since he could not concentrate on anything. The baby needed to be continuously looked after, even when she was sleeping.

Even getting to the bank or going to the post office was a big problem for Oguebe.

Each of these visits would involve kitting up the baby and carrying her on her car-seat.

On one occasion Oguebe had braved going to the post office with the baby to send out some certified mails. The walk from the car park to the inside of the post office was so burdensome with the baby carried along on one hand in the car-seat.

Oguebe had never realized how heavy seven-month-old Baby Lydia had grown. He had to drop the car-seat on two occasions along the pedestrian walk-way to rest his hands. He was wondering aloud whether it was merely the extra weight of the car seat that made the load so heavy.

The return visit to Boston was with Nena who had come visiting to Sunderland.
Baby Lydia was crawling all over the place. It was more fun for Oguebe and Agesi.
Another person was looking after the baby while Grandpa and Grandma were observers.
It was great relief after three uninterrupted weeks of baby-sitting in Sunderland.
"I now appreciate the great role that baby-sitters play. We were once, getting surprised at what we considered as exorbitant fees that were charged by professional baby-sitters.
We now know that they deserve even more than the two thousand dollars a month that the least exorbitant of them charges." Oguebe said.
"But you remember that our friends Phil and Naomi in New York paid their live-in nanny two thousand and five hundred dollars a month and we said it was far too costly." Agesi said.
"Yes, we thought the pay of baby-sitters was too high. But that was before we became temporary baby-sitters. I guess we now know better." Oguebe said, almost resignedly.
"Yes indeed!" Agesi said. "Where it is possible, the job of baby-sitting should be left only for family members who are not doing it for the pay.
It should preferably be done by people who would do it for the love of the baby.
It should be done by family members or close friends who would do it for loved ones.

It should not be left for commercial nannies whose emotional stability cannot always be guaranteed and who naturally may occasionally not withstand the shenanigans, the fretting and the whining of little babies.

It should preferably be left for people like us, grandpas and grandmas, who do it for the babies that we love, our grandchildren whose cry would appear like pin pricks to our skins and whose pain would appear like daggers to our hearts.

Excepting the mother and father of a child, who else can feel more the cry or discomfort of any baby than the grandparents? Who, more than Grandpa and Grandma, can better share in the discomfort or pains of the crying little infant? Who but them will be prepared to make the ultimate sacrifice for a baby where the need absolutely arises? There is no gainsaying that many professional nannies are very good and exceptionally loyal to their wards, but a hireling almost always remains a hireling while the good shepherd will be prepared to lay down his life for his flock as stated in the Holy Books.

In many circumstances commercial nannies are inevitably employed. In such circumstances the pay should be so good that it will be too attractive to toy with. Where a commercial nanny is inevitably hired, the pay should be very attractive. Thus, there will be very little room for discontent. That way alone, can parents ensure that their loved ones are in relatively safe hands.

Even when love of a baby by a nanny is not something that can be bought, very attractive conditions of service for the nanny will at least ensure a good measure of attachment to the baby who is the most dependent among us." Grandpa Oguebe concluded

"Yes," Agesi said. "It is only people who do it as a labor of love and not for pay, who can most effectively baby-sit little babies. Even though many nannies have great love for the babies that they care for, no amount of remuneration can effectively compensate for the sacrifices that are entailed in baby-sitting."

Nena listened with rapt attention as her parents discussed. It was obvious that their new roles, though exciting, were nonetheless physically stressful. She felt the need to chip in a word of encouragement.

"Dad and Mom, don't worry about the hassles. Baby Lydia will pay you back many times over with love when she grows up." Nena chipped in, as if to commiserate with the embattled grandparents.

"No, Nena, it is not all about the payment. That's exactly what we are talking about. It is all a labor of love. Besides, Baby Lydia is already paying us back multiple times over by the mere joy and fulfilment that she brings to our lives. She is such a joy to behold. Her mere smile each time makes our day." Agesi said.

"It is just that sometimes one feels imprisoned inside the house. And she creeps into all sorts of hidden places in the house making it mandatory that an eye must be kept on her at all times when she is awake. I wish she had started walking, so that sometimes she can accompany me to a few places and walk from the car to the house, instead of being always carried." Oguebe said

"The young shall grow, dad. Baby Lydia is making great progress. You remember that only a couple of months ago, that she could not even sit upright unsupported. In a matter of months, she will be running and you can take her along with you to the parks." Nena said holding up Baby Lydia's little hands. Baby Lydia smiled broadly as if she understood what was being said about her.

Agesi enjoyed the drive to Boston, sitting comfortably on the passenger's seat while Oguebe drove. That was the first time in many weeks that she had the luxury of relaxing in the passenger's seat without having to watch over Baby Lydia while her husband was on the steering. The drive to Boston appeared to have lasted a shorter time than usual because of the relaxed mood.

Oguebe and Agesi had never had the luxury of surveying their surroundings in the Boston neighborhood where Nena lived. The area was called Harbor-Point and was in the Boston area of Dorchester. 'Harbor-Point Apartments' was a very beautiful gated community with many relatively tasty rental apartments. The biggest attraction of Harbor-Point was that it bordered the Bay and the view of the Ocean was very spectacular. At the early stages of Oguebe and Agesi's visits to Nena, they hardly had the time to visit the Bay Area. They only learnt from Nena that it was a beautiful area. They had never seen the many facilities like the swimming pool area, the gym, the numerous relaxation spots along the ocean view. They only saw the tennis court from inside the car as they drove by.

At the latter visit to Boston the grandparents from rural Sunderland had the opportunity of taking an early Sunday morning walk along the Bay. It was a most fascinating view.

From the Harbor-Point end of the Bay, Oguebe and Agesi could see the many jet planes that landed at, or took off from the Logan Airport in the distance. They could see a number of ships that docked or took off from the distance. They could see a wooded island that jutted out from the middle of the ocean. It looked like a new-day medusa erupting from the vast blue sea.

The waves of water beating against the giant granite boulders that lined the Bay were a joy to behold. The scores of seagulls and ocean ducks that darted against the waves and picked up some washed-up worms and other prey could keep a visitor glued on a spot for hours on end.

Oguebe and Agesi had planned to traverse the entire length of the Bay area that bordered on Harbor Point Apartments. But Oguebe, a great lover of Nature easily got so glued to a particular spot that after more than one hour on the Bay, the couple had not covered more than two dozen yards of the beautifully-paved walk way along the Bay.

Many joggers were seen equally enjoying the view along the Bay in Harbor-Point. It was a world of its own, a scenery which many of the residents of the area, just like Nena before then, might not have fully appreciated. It was perhaps only the likes of Oguebe and Agesi who were only visiting who might fully appreciate the beauty and the grandeur of the beautiful neighborhood that was called Harbor-Point Apartments in Boston Massachusetts.

Oguebe and Agesi spent more than three hours along the Bay. Even Agesi who was not as Nature-crazy as Oguebe did not complain about the long outing. The couple intermittently rested in the many designated paved areas along the Bay. Some of the areas were open while some others were covered. But the entire place was kept sparklingly clean and there were appropriately-positioned metal and wooden benches for any weary legs. Short history of the Harbor Point and Boston was carved out in stone intermittently along the shore, adding to the beauty of the tour and educational enrichment of the numerous visitors to the place.

"I wish we could bring Baby Lydia with us to this place. You remember how excited she was the first time we took her out to the Open Spaces in Sunderland? She certainly would have loved to see these ducks and sea gulls." Oguebe said.

"Don't you think she is still too young to appreciate these sceneries?" Agesi said.

"No, I believe that babies know and appreciate things much more than we imagine. Don't you see how excited she is when she sees other young babies? You remember how she beamed with smiles at those two babies that attended her Baptismal ceremony? I believe young babies know quite a bit, it is only that they can't express their feelings in speech." Oguebe said.

"Perhaps it would have been a good thing to have a way of knowing what is within the minds of little babies. Child psychologists and neuroscientists may have to work harder in these regards." Agesi said.

"How did you get to know about this place?" Oguebe asked Nena when the two grandparents got back to their daughter's apartment.

"A friend recommended it to me. At first I thought the rents were on the high side until I moved around and found the amenities." Nena said.

'It is a great place. It is worth whatever you are paying per month." Oguebe said.

"You mean even if it is ten thousand dollars per month for one apartment?"

"No, even if it is three thousand dollars per month for your two-bed room apartment."

"Well I am certainly not paying up to that."

"Then it is a great price. It is really a great neighborhood to live in." Oguebe said.

The Sunday service at the nearby Catholic Church was particularly fulfilling after the refreshing walk through the ocean front.

Baby Lydia looked radiant in her new cream-colored Sunday dress. It was her first Sunday service in Boston in the previous three months. As of her last attendance at the church, she was not yet as aware of her environments as she had become in her most recent visit to Boston. She was very alert and kept gazing from person to person in the church. She received lots of compliments from close-by worshippers with her unique light brown complexion, round large eyes and ready and amiable smiles. She had been fully fed on milk and cereals just before leaving the house and with fresh diaper change and the warm arms of a loving mom, she was all smiles, flapping her palms and appearing to want to participate in the church hymns. Nothing could be more fulfilling for Grandma and Grandpa than the sight of a healthy and happy baby granddaughter participating in a church service during a weekend away from home.

During the general-greetings stage of the church service, Baby Lydia's eyeballs darted curiously from person to person as the traditional handshakes were exchanged. As some worshippers waved hands to worshippers sitting far from them, Baby Lydia appeared to understand that it was greeting time. She flapped her left hand vigorously, though incoherently, as if in consonance with the other worshippers. This apparent show of camaraderie from an eight-month baby elicited multiple reciprocity from a dozen and more members of the congregation, to Baby Lydia.

Outside the church hall, when the service was over, photo-enthusiast Grandpa took many snapshots of the young lady of the house for enrichment of the family album.

As Grandma entered back into the car at the end of the church service, Baby Lydia appeared to want to stay back in the church premises. She kicked her legs and started crying loudly. Feeling that something was hurting the baby, Grandma quickly came out of the car to check. Once out of the car, back into where she was seeing other church-attendees, the little lady immediately ceased crying. Having apparently pacified the baby, Grandma went back again with Baby Lydia. The crying re-started in earnest. It indeed increased in crescendo with kicking and pulling at anything that was within reach.

It soon became obvious that the little lady did not want to go home.

The grandparents and surprised mom had to stand outside the car and watch other church-attendees depart one by one. Finally, it was only the reverend minister standing outside the church. As the latter waved at the Oguebe party and went back into the church hall, a final move to get back Baby Lydia into the car quietly was made. It was only then that the little lady settled down into her car seat without crying and kicking. She obviously knew that the party was over.

The little lady's need for excitement and company was becoming obvious. She certainly needed to start day-care so that she would interact with other kids her age.

Chapter 18

LEARNING ACROSS THREE GENERATIONS

Learning and re-learning were going on across the three generations;
Little Baby Lydia was learning the art of surviving in a strange world of daily-unfolding novelties, complete dependence and family love.
Nena was learning the art of motherhood even as she battled with the challenges of medical school education.
Grandma and Grandpa, Nena's parents, on their part were relearning a long-forgotten art of changing diapers, childcare and baby-sitting, with the attendant joys and challenges.
For Grandma and Grandpa, each new day of baby-sitting Baby Lydia, was a fresh reminder of the rather cumbersome, yet sweet memories of a distant past in child care. And it was a distant, yet very vivid past where disposable diapers were not in use; a past where the tell-tale sign of a baby in the house usually was the conspicuous display in the early morning sunlight, of rows and rows of washed white cotton baby napkins which were usually spread on railings or strings in front of the house for them to dry to be reused. Those were the days of reusable baby diapers. As the diapers were soiled they were heaped together in baskets or basins and washed periodically with detergent and bleach, perhaps once a day, perhaps twice.

More often than not, in those Agesi and Oguebe child-bearing days, those napkins were hand-washed and hand-rinsed, sometimes in locations where there was no pipe-borne water or electricity. Obviously, there were nothing like washers or dryers in existence, and so, all washing of soiled clothing was done by hand. Those were those distant days which neither Nena nor Baby Lydia, nor anybody in their respective generations would possibly imagine, much less witness.

But Grandma and Grandpa still remembered. And as they reminisced, they wondered how they and the young parents of those days were able to cope with the challenges of baby sanitation and child-rearing.

Notwithstanding the prevailing modernity and the advent of disposable diapers, Grandma and Grandpa still needed some re-learning and adaptation. They re-learnt that having to regularly change a baby's diapers was not an easy task.

Grandma had largely forgotten how tiny and fragile little babies could be. Grandpa did not forget. No, he simply had not experienced it at all, and so, he simply did not know. His, was a generation where the man of the house left for work in the morning to make the money for the family upkeep, while the infant was asleep and came home at night when the infant had gone to bed. And mom, or mom and a house-help nurtured the infant.

For Nena, the learning experience was on-going. Being in school in a rigorous medical program with very few, if any other mothers in the class, she could only learn from what mom taught at home on the few days a week that the latter was available from an equally rigorous medical practice in a distant city.

Whatever else Nena learnt were either from books, from the few pre-natal instruction classes she attended, from occasional home health visits graciously organized by the state authorities, but largely from on-the-spot experience. And more often than not, the best of the teachings were the things that she learnt by practical experience.

Nena was to learn that feeding a baby required technique. She was to learn that the art which was often taken for granted required patience, gentility and utmost care. The small mouth that would receive the mother's nipple or the teat of a feeding bottle, could be sucking ineffectually or it could be sucking in excess. If sucking ineffectually, the baby could simply be sucking air. Thereafter she would be full, but not with food, but with flatus. She would bloat the tommy and cry uncontrollably because of trapped gas.

If on the other hand she was sucking in excess, she could gulp too much milk within a very short time. This of course would induce vomiting and there might even be danger of choking.

And so, Nena as a young mom, needed to learn the techniques of child care, so there would be fewer mistakes.

Nena was also to learn that the persistent cry of that fully-fed infant could mean one or more of several things. She needed to learn to distinguish between the cry from hunger, from bloating, from wetness or even from the cry of wanting to sleep.

And the little bundle of joy could easily swing from one mood to another, with little or no warnings and simply within seconds of each other. You took her up she cried; you brought her down she cried; you held her to your chest she cried; and you placed her on her cot she cried the more. And she cried so hard that you wondered who the persecutor could be.

Who, or what was it that was hurting her?

Was it you, or was it the tiny stockings on her little feet?
Was it the dress that she wore that hurt?
Was it the diapers that you had only just then changed; or was it the protective beep that you put around her neck?
Even the little rubber soother that was called a "pacifier" would not pacify her.
But a little gentle rocking could do the trick.
Carrying her across your shoulder and walking around could be of help.
A little rhythm that accompanied the rocking could finally sooth Baby Lydia to a transient sleep.
And as she momentarily shut her tear-filled eyes to catch momentary sleep, Baby Lydia would still sob.
And when there was no pacifier in her mouth she would still suck her lips.
Sucking reflex by babies must really be a compelling force!

Laying Baby Lydia in bed to sleep was expected to bring relief. If she could sleep for an hour or two, Nena could catch some sleep too. Or she could attend to some urgent class assignment. And Grandma and Grandpa could also relax for a while and rest their arms.
But resting in bed still had its flaws.
Anxiety and fears accompanied every step.
The several dangers associated with babies in their cots always came to mind.
It was so difficult not to intermittently imagine the worst.
Even when all known precautions were by all parties well observed
It was difficult to completely abolish from the mind, some stories of woes.
Yet, amidst human anxiety, fears or silly apprehension

The joys of motherhood were joys like no other.

The pride of being grandparents appeared to top them all.
Watching one's children grow was great pleasures on its own.
But watching grandchildren grow was fascination like no other.
The children of one's children were like many for the price of one.
And the pleasure of seeing them grow was one that could not be readily imagined.

As the little baby slept she still needed some care.
Even when the bed was well-secured, redundant clothing and linen must be well-tucked in. If not well-tucked in, they might as well be entirely eliminated.
Nena's pediatric lecture on Sudden Infant Death Syndrome often came up dreadfully in her mind.
Therefore, the baby's beddings must never be loose.
And, all possible causes of suffocation must be kept away. The watchful eyes of the mother or the babysitter must remain ever like the eagle's.

For Baby Lydia every new day appeared to confer new knowledge and maturity.
It was either in facial recognition, mastery of the environment or in recognition of her daily routines.
Even with regards to her feeding she daily matured.

Keeping track of Baby Lydia as she grew past nine months became more challenging.
Yes, it became more challenging, yet more exciting.
She would get under odd places and cover herself with anything within reach.
She would grab at any loose clothing, any hanging curtains, any pillows or bedcovers.

She would do hide and seek with herself, covering her face on and off and grinning in the process
She would pull at table covers, fumble with electrical sockets and grab and try to chew at dangling wires! Even when sockets were taped or sealed off, she would readily get attracted to those unwanted places. She enjoyed getting as close as possible to the TV screen,
And she (understandably) wanted to watch from a foot or two away.
The closer the preferable by her baby lens. But that closer, the more potentially harmful to her health especially her tender eyes.

Dissuasion from the TV appeared as purposeful deprivation to her.
And she would protest when pulled away or when the TV was put off.
And as she got to one year and older, she would pick up any remote or what looked like a remote.
And she would point the latter in the direction of the TV and expect it to respond without the "on" button. Only the sound of "Five Little Ducks" from her toy in the play-pan would serve for distraction.
Even when other children TV alternatives were provided, what Mom and Grandma watched were the most attractive to her. Even when she understood no word of what was being said, she still gazed. It was only much later, after 15 months, that children TV programs and cartoons began to attract her.

Children's books were much fun,
But the pages would be repeatedly turned and vigorously pulled at.
And the sturdy books would be tossed repeatedly up and down.

Thick and toughly-bound, those books endured most assaults.

But when they were bitten at and chewed, they often succumbed to saliva and the pull of those very sharp baby teeth.

Yes, the teeth that bit at the pages were few but they were incredibly sharp.

And the pages would be well coated with copious saliva before being chewed at.

The pages might not have been read, but they proved very useful in the end.

They certainly served as momentary distractions too.

They also were good introduction to baby's learning world.

And the distraction that they provided could not be underestimated.

Chapter 19

AS UBIQUITOUS AS ONE COULD BE

The job of babysitting grew more intensive by the day after the first nine months. Baby Lydia was all over the place crawling on her knees. She would grip at objects and stand as she pleased. The speed of her crawling could only best be seen rather than imagined. She could crawl faster on her knees than she could have done running on her feet.

"Will Baby Lydia ever have the urge to walk? She appears so comfortable on her knees that she may not want to stand and walk." Grandpa mused.

And with the crawling, came extra risks of injury. She would crawl up to small crevices and commence pulling at anything within reach.
She crawled up to the bed and pulled down the sheets.
She crawled up to the electronics on stands in the living room and started pulling at the electrical cords.
On a beautiful Saturday morning after she was dressed up to travel to Boston, she crept up to the table and reached for a barely-visible cord of the ceramic electric table lamp and briskly pulled on the cord!
The crashing collapse and shattering of the giant ceramic lamp-holder attracted the attention of Grandma and Grandpa to the scene of the lamp holder. The beautiful ceramic lamp-holder had been smashed into one score pieces and more.

The heavy pot perhaps barely missed crashing onto the head of the "culprit". She apparently was not scared or shaken by the shattering noise. She was busy pointing at the broken pieces and muttering "ta, ta, ta".
She appeared to be asking the ceramic pot why it broke!

Grandma soon arrived at the scene. Horrified at what she saw, she spontaneously shouted "Baby Lydia!".
At the loud and apparently harsh shouting of her name, the little wrecker of the ornamental beautiful lamp-holder immediately broke into a cry of protest.
"Why do you shout my name angrily?" She appeared to be saying in silent protest.
"I only multiplied one object into a hundred and more objects!" She appeared to be saying in her hysterical cry.
Yes, indeed, the little princess had turned one ceramic toy into a dozen and more manageable toys, each useful only to a fairly princess! The little princess probably had expected a smile and perhaps some words of praise from Grandma, on the latter's visualization of the good work that she had done. It was perhaps only at the harsh shouting of her name, did the little princess realize that she had done something terrible. She had broken Grandma's treasured ceramic lamp-holder into a dozen and more useless pieces!
But she must not be scolded!

Why would anyone dare to scold a little princess for breaking a mere ceramic lamp holder?
"No, no, no! Baby girl, no crying! Grandma will beat up the ceramic lamp-holder for breaking in front of you.

It should not have disrupted your peace and your play!" Grandma pleaded, if only to placate the crying little princess.
And the crying stopped only after Grandma had beaten up, or pretended to be beating up, the broken lamp-holder.
"You, nasty lamp-holder, never you ever make my baby cry again!" Grandma told the broken lamp-holder as she beat up the little pieces with the palm of her hand.
Even as young as she was, Baby Lydia watched and listened. And she appeared to have been appeased by Grandma beating up the object that made her cry!
And as soon as she was let loose on the floor once again, the search for other objects to break resumed in earnest.

Anything and all loose things that lay within grabbing reach needed to evacuate.
They must evacuate or they risked destruction.
Only a large toy-filled room with everything on the floor would be allowed to remain intact.
Every other thing must yield or be made to yield.

Baby Lydia had learnt new tricks by her eleventh month.
She had inadvertently rolled down from the sofa in the living room a couple of times.
On each of the occasions she had cried briefly and was never really hurt.
Nobody initially knew that she had matured into climbing back into the sofa until she was seen falling off it a second time within a few minutes.
Luckily the sofa was low enough not to have much traumatic effects on the playful little lady.

Yes, Baby Lydia had learnt to climb onto the sofa. She must have surreptitiously practiced several times, the art of lifting one knee up the sofa which she would grab tenaciously with both hands. She would then lift the rest of her trunk and swing upwards and land her trunk on the seat with a broad smile for the feat so achieved. It appeared relatively easy for her to climb on top of the sofa, once the first successful attempt was made.

But for her to come down from the sofa was initially a problem.

She was seen attempting to climb down head-first with her hands outstretched.

Grandpa was shocked when he first saw Baby Lydia attempting to climb down from the sofa.

"We must not put Baby on top of the sofa and leave the place, I just saw her attempting to climb down from where she had been placed", Grandpa told Agesi and Nena.

"But I did not put her up there, dad" Nena said.

"And I didn't either", Agesi also said.

"Then who put Baby Lydia up the sofa?"

Grandpa had then brought down Baby Lydia and had left her on the carpet.

As the older folks argued about who put Baby Lydia up the sofa, Baby Lydia was seen to again clamber up the sofa, very effortlessly. And as she got on the sofa she giggled out loudly as if to mock the adults who had underestimated her abilities and who were still busy arguing about who put her up there!

It was like magic to Agesi and Oguebe. No member of the family had before imagined that Baby Lydia was able to climb up the sofa.

A new challenge therefore arose as to how to guard against the baby falling off the sofa when no one was looking.

Pillows were thereafter lined on the floor along all the sofas. These were to break her fall or give Baby Lydia soft landing when she would fall.

But Baby Lydia on her own had learnt the tricks. She would reverse herself on getting to the edge of the sofa. Her legs ordinarily would not easily reach the ground. But she would slide down legs-first and then land on her outstretched toes.

The pillows then needed to be removed to provide good landing balance. It was amazing what an eleven-month-old could do! How innovative; how very fascinating!

"The reasoning ability of man is truly great!" Oguebe said.

"Even as early as at one year, the human's abilities to judge consequences of many actions are really immense. Otherwise how did Baby Lydia know that she must not tumble down from the sofa head-on?" Agesi again queried herself.

Little babies must be more capable than even the wildest imaginations of adults could conjure.

Nobody taught Baby Lydia the danger that landing on her head might involve.

Landing on her head was, to her, not an option.

Legs might hang up in the air but eventually they would reach the ground.

The assurance that that would happen was not given by anyone but was imagined by the baby.

And the art of sliding down the sofa was done with all self-assurance and with gentility.

It must not be done as fast as with crawling.

The destinations in crawling and in getting down a bed, respectively, were different.
But they were learnt by intuition.

Many more things were learnt by Baby Lydia between the ninth and twelfth months.
The oral stage which reached peak six months earlier, had started to ebb. Objects that were picked up by hand were better scrutinized between both hands.
They would thereafter be either flung around as toys or were thrust into the mouth.
"Big girls" of one year, like Baby Lydia, were not silly enough to thrust anything and everything into their mouths.
They had become more selective but not perfect, about what should, or should not enter their mouths.
The big girl could pick up a crawling ant from the floor during a crawling routine. They might turn the live ant round and round in their hands. They would not let it go. But certainly, they would be very reluctant to thrust the nasty live object into their mouths.

But the big girl could pick up some carelessly-dropped food crumb from the floor. And after turning it round and round in her tiny palms, she would thrust the old food crumb into her mouth. Only when Mom or Grandpa or Grandma observed the chewing movement of the lips would the object be assessed and removed.
And so, if Mom or Grandpa or Grandma was not attentive enough to observe consumption of any obnoxious object, the little lady could make a snack out of a dead ant, a dead roach or another dead insect!

Perhaps the Big Girl's sharp eyes and her sharp sense of smell would very soon help her to distinguish between what was once thought to be edible and what was not.

At twelve months, the Big Girl chose what not to pick up from the floor. But once she picked up anything that was carelessly left on the floor she might play with the same for a while. But the object might eventually end up being thrust into her mouth.

But Baby Lydia was able to distinguish between what should be chewed as food and what would merely be inserted into the mouth and bitten at, as a toy.

How surprising to observe Baby Lydia chew her food? With eight teeth, four upper and four lower incisors, Baby Lydia interestingly bit off and chewed her food.

How interesting to watch four upper and four lower erupted teeth work synchronously with the posterior gums to grind soft meat and cookies!

Baby Lydia would occasionally tear to pieces any paper within reach. She appeared to be particularly in love with pieces of paper.

She would chew loose paper but would hardly swallow any bit.

Yes, she knew what to chew and swallow and what to chew and retain in her mouth!

The edges of paper boxes would be chewed but would never be swallowed.

What she saw adults eating were readily recognized as food.

Just as the kid of a goat watched its mother chew, the human baby often watched the parents chew and swallow.

And the human baby like the young of goats, learnt more by imitation.

And Baby Lydia learnt even faster than her adult family members could imagine.

And as she chewed the food, Baby Lydia knew when it was soft enough to be swallowed.

And if she inserted tough or fibrous meat into her mouth she knew not to swallow it.
She indeed would pull out tough fibrous meat out of her mouth when she knew she could not pulverize it well enough.
And she knew not to accept more food when she still had food in her mouth. She would turn her head away even from the most delicious food if she already had food in her mouth when the delicious new food was offered. She would discard any food remaining in her mouth before accepting any new food.

The development of the human person was so very fascinating to observe. And watching Baby Lydia mature as a baby was such a treasure.
It was so very educative; so very fascinating!

The development and maturity of the young human being makes the adult human appreciate better the deep mystery that is humankind.
From birth to adulthood the human mystery unfolds.
From the bubbling mature man to the wheel-chair-bound Shakespearean Seventh Age
The mystery of man beats all wonders known to man.
What an awesome creator the Maker of Man must be.
What an awesome architect and innovator He truly is!

In watching Baby Lydia grow, Grandma and Grandpa once again truly saw the face and wonders of God.
When they had their own baby, perhaps they were either too young, too naïve or too unappreciative of Nature. They, therefore, had probably taken too many things for granted.

But as grandparents being very close and watching the day to day development of a grandchild, they were able to appreciate the incredible and fascinating stages of human development. And these constituted a most enduring course of events and experience which no amount of abstract teaching could render. Grandma and Grandpa came to realize more than ever before the truism in their favorite church song, Carl Boberg's "How Great Thou Art".

At diners it was such joy for Grandma and Grandpa to watch Baby Lydia perching on her high-chair and picking up and eating her food spread out on her tray. And what constituted the food was mostly soft puffs and mashed vegetable meant for kids.
All that was hot or very spicy was kept away.
Any bit of the food could find its way to the eyes.
And the crying would get all diners doing rubber-necking.
And Mom and Grandma would get some blaming.
All that might attract unnecessary attention was a no-no.
And nuts and bone-spicules were completely out of bounds.
Even on the adult menu for the day, the latter were avoided.
No chances were taken with Little Baby Lydia at diner.

And Nena watched with enthusiasm and joy as her baby fed herself.
The little morsels were put into the mouth as clumsily as the action might be.
Half of the food fell off back into the tray or off to the ground.
Half of the remaining half was smeared on the hair, on the dress and around the face.

But the little that was left, found its way gripped by the clumsy fingers into the mouth.

The eyes were avoided and the ears and nostrils did not receive the morsels.
Only the mouth opened wide on contact, to receive the food.
And the coordination, though poor, was just too fascinating to watch!
Has anyone imagined who it was that taught the little baby to feed herself?
Again, has any asked why it was, that the food was not put into the nostrils or the ears?
Has it ever occurred to any, why and how babies learnt?
What was taken for granted in the development of a little baby was in its entirety a great mystery.

We simply called it "reflexes" or "intuition".
And the wonders of indomitable Nature got belittled.
And the glory that was God's thus got so diminished.
And we all assumed that learning would inevitably accompany maturity in all circumstances.
But close observation of developing Baby Lydia by Grandpa and Grandma, forever magnified the creator.
And the unfathomable greatness of the Maker of man could never be fully comprehended.
Compartmentalizing the mystery that is man into religious cubicles is a great disservice to the Maker of the universe.
Denial of a great coordinating hand in the existence of the universe in itself is an even greater tragedy.
Science and religion need not collide in disagreement in a situation so straightforward.
"Nothing comes from nothing, nothing ever could."
Perhaps it required a Friar Maria in the "Sound of Music" to remind Agesi and Oguebe of this truism.

And these, so obviously manifested in Little Baby Lydia, as she daily developed.

Observing Little Baby Lydia developing, readily brought to the fore, the mysteries of creation and development.

Only the good fortune of being a baby-sitting grandpa and a baby-sitting grandma could offer the latter in abundance.

Again the food might be mostly-scattered on her tray as Baby Lydia fed herself.

Yes, half or more of the food might have found itself on the floor.

As the tiny fingers grabbed the food particles, the back of the clenched fist might find itself in the mouth while most of the actual food would drop off the unclenched fist.

Some of the food will inevitably find itself into the mouth and the chewing with the front teeth and the gums at the back ridges would commence.

Nothing was more intriguing than seeing Little Baby Lydia at the early stages of learning to feed herself.

Nothing would be more fascinating for any grandparent to witness.

It was Nature and human development at their best.

The joy was immense seeing a daughter and a granddaughter live their lives.

Seeing the tiny baby of yesterday feeding herself today was such joy to behold.

Ever wondered why they are called "Bouncing Baby Girl" and "Bouncing Baby Boy"?

Grandpa was astounded by how Baby Lydia could bounce up and down in her cot.

She also tried to bounce as high on the carpeted wooden floor. It was amazing how she did not appear to feel the pains of a hard floor as she sprang up and down on her thighs without the cushioning effect of a mattress.

Yet she bounced up and down the carpet and the wooden floor but with measured force.

Bouncing baby boys and bouncing baby girls truly bounced!

And the joy that they brought with their laughter was ever so enchanting.

And the reflection on the mysteries of growth and development were even more enchanting.

Chapter 20

THE FIRST FALTERING STEPS

Baby Lydia would bounce up and down as high as six inches off the bed with her legs crossed. She immediately recognized the difference between a springy mattress and the hard ground. On the former, she would bounce up and down repeatedly, sometimes up to ten times at a stretch. On a hard ground however, she would bounce with measured force only two or three times at a stretch.
 Even without her hands on the ground to lift her off the ground she would bounce!
It was amazing how she could lift her entire frame off the ground effortlessly and several times at a stretch. And thereafter, she would exhibit little or no panting. A good measurement on the percentage of health and life, may well lie with a measure of the degree of ability to bounce, or lift oneself off the ground without support from the hands!

The broad smile of contentment that beamed on Little Baby Lydia's face each time she finished bouncing might well be a confirmation of the full measure of good health and full life that abounded in her. She obviously manifested a deserved glow of achievement after the bouts of bouncing.
Ever watched a giant frog leap? Those powerful thigh muscles that propel the amphibian into the air must have found great resemblance in bouncing baby boys and girls.

At twelve months, Baby Lydia would hold things and walk freely around the room. Occasionally she would forget to hold things and stand on her own and try to take a step forward without realizing that she was not holding on anything. Only when she appeared to realize that she was not holding at something would she fall back into a squatting position. Obviously, she was fed up with crawling on the floor. But she had not mustered the courage to utilize her strong leg muscles to take continuous steps forward. The fear of falling apparently held her back.

Thus, it was that Baby Lydia practiced walking about with support for close to three months. On her first birthday she had perfected getting anywhere she wanted to go to in the living room, holding onto any objects that came handy, cushions, side stools, tables and so on. But she would not stand unaided for longer than a few seconds. She appeared too afraid of falling without support.

Mom, Grandma and Grandpa were beginning to worry whether Baby Lydia would only walk holding on to things; so comfortable was she getting briskly around but only with support. Grandpa and Grandma had almost forgotten their experiences with children around them. They had almost forgotten that one of their neighbors' sons crawled for so long that even at eighteen months he was still crawling with little or no effort to stand unsupported, much more, walk. The latter crawled for so long and over such long and rough distances along the corridors that his knees were occasionally sore from crawling on concrete paved surfaces outside the house. And he would often strip off his pants and crawl bare-legged and bruise his knees. It got so bad that the neighbors had considered putting on paddings on their son's knees to prevent bruises.

But that was three decades and more earlier. And Grandpa and Grandma had naturally forgotten their own experiences and what they witnessed with their neighbors.

From thirteen months, even in spite of their professional backgrounds, Grandpa and Grandma had started worrying about Baby Lydia being all over the place but "refusing to walk".
Nena herself had no experience except from the milestones that she read from books.
"My friend Theresa's daughter walked exactly on her first birthday. And Baby Lydia is thirteen months and she is not walking!" Nena lamented.
"Why doesn't Baby Lydia want to walk?" She asked.
"Different babies behave differently as regards milestones, Nena. Baby Lydia will walk at her own time". Agesi tried to reassure Nena, even in spite of her own hidden concerns about perceived delay in Baby Lydia's milestones.

It was exactly at fourteen months and two days of age that Nena came out of her room to the corridor that led to the kitchen. Lo and behold, Little Baby Lydia was there playing with her toys. On sighting her mom, the little lady got up from where she was playing with her toys and, holding on to the wall at first, but later freely, started walking towards her mom!
She walked with staggering steps.
She walked with outstretched hands.
She walked as if every step would see her fall.
Hurrah! At last, Little baby Lydia had started walking!
She took six steps before she fell forward on her hands!
But she had started walking all the same.

Again, Little baby Lydia had started walking!

It took a little longer time than expected.
Every day after her first birthday, Mom, Grandma and Grandpa had looked out.
Daily, they expected to see those first steps.
But they came on at last, and without any warnings or any prodding.
Nena shouted with amazement and great joy.
It was at her shouting that Baby Lydia went down on her hands.
Perhaps she should have been left to walk further without celebration. But the amazement and excitement were well worth a shout.

Who would not get excited at the first walk of her angel?
Who would not celebrate at a pleasant surprise from a loving daughter?
Who would not shout with joy on seeing her daughter's first upright walk in life?

Baby Lydia was at last fully upright on her legs!
She had allayed any and all fears about any developmental delays.
She would henceforth not have to walk on all fours like "the lower mammals".
She would henceforth walk upright like all humans.
And Nena was justified in giving a shout of joy.
She would no longer imagine her daughter "walking like a chimpanzee". She had used the latter words in describing her fears about the apparent delay in her daughter's first walk.

After that first walk, there was no going back by Baby Lydia.
Yes, she stumbled forward at the shout from her mom.

But she immediately got back on her feet and continued her upright walk.
For the following four or five days, she still staggered and stretched out her hands as she walked.
But by the end of the first week, the little lady had almost perfected.
There was no going back once the breakthrough had been made.

It happened so suddenly but it soon was the new normal.
And Baby Lydia savored every moment of walking upright without support
She displayed her new feat at every opportunity.
And she developed a new song as she walked around the room.
"Ta! Ta! Ta!" was a new song.
And it accompanied every footstep along the walk.
Even when nobody understood what she said, she still babbled.

"I can now walk around like every other person", she seemed to be saying.
"I can walk, and very soon I will run.
Why have I been crawling on my knees?
Sitting still like a dummy and gathering dirt on my dress.
Now I can get around as I please.
I can swing my arms and reach up the table tops like Mom and Grandma."

Sure, as stated, after some three weeks of starting to walk, Little Baby Lydia was running around the house.
Yes, a small obstacle on her path could cause her to trip over.
And she swung around her arms for balance as she stamped her little feet on the floor.

But she was walking all the same. And the reverberations of her steps were heard as any other's. It was a big transformation, truly very worthy of thanksgiving.

Chapter 21

THE FIRST FEVER;
THE JITTERS FEVER

It had appeared all so smooth-sailing.
Baby Lydia had not been a voracious eater. But she was usually enthusiastic about food especially when she was allowed to play intermittently with the food in the bottle or on her new high-chair tray.
Since she graduated to taking semi solid foods on a regular basis, at about eight months of age, Baby Lydia's frequency of milk intake had reduced to two or three times a day as opposed to her previous four to six hourly intakes.

It was usually great fun watching Little Baby Lydia feeding from her high chair to which she was usually securely strapped. At first, she would sit gently in the high chair and kick her legs with joy on seeing the plate of her food being lowered into the tray of the high chair. She would initially consent to morsels of food being put into her mouth. She would open her mouth wide like a nestling bird being fed by its mother. At a later stage she started rejecting being mouth-fed like a little girl. No, she had become a "big girl". And big girls were not mouth-fed. They fed themselves. And so, at this latter stage, Baby Lydia would feed herself.

She would stretch out her fingers and clumsily dip into the plate of food. She would gather as much of the food as possible and shove everything, food and fingers into her mouth!

In the process most of the food would fall off. But even if only the equivalent of half a grain of rice got into the mouth, the big girl would still be glad and chew. At least she was feeding herself. That was the stage at which the little lady was, when she was taken to her first diner.

The mouth-feeding or self-feeding would last for only as long as Baby Lydia's patience lasted. Thereafter, the scattering of the food would start.

And the scattering would be performed so briskly and so viciously as if the little lady had been at war with the food.

Again, Little Baby Lydia had never had a fever up until her first birthday.

She was a healthy baby, strong, and developing by the day. Her immunization schedule was strictly adhered to. Nena had been pouring encomiums on Grandpa and Grandma for Nena's good health and sound development.

"She has never fallen ill, not even a mild fever. Grandma and Grandpa have done a good job on you, Baby Lydia", Nena had said to Baby Lydia while gently rocking her up and down her thighs.

The family was dressed up to dine out that evening. They were encouraged to take Little Baby Lydia out again to diner after her impressive performance at the first diner.

Grandma had momentarily carried Baby Lydia on her shoulders, ready to put her on her car seat.

"It looks like her forehead is unusually hot, Nena"
Agesi said, feeling Baby Lydia's brow with the palms of
her hand.
"And she is not as agile as she used to be." Agesi
further stated.
"Perhaps that is because she has not taken her usual
afternoon nap. She often knows when we all are about
to go out with her. And she feels very excited. Perhaps
after she sleeps a little in the car she will be her usual
self again." Nena said as she raised Baby Lydia's gown
and felt her skin-temperature with the hand at the
back of the baby's neck.
"You are very right, mom, baby's body is unusually
hot. And her eye-lids appear a little droopy." Nena
said immediately looking scared.
"And she has never had a fever. Wow! This is
strange!" Nena said.
As Nena dashed into her room to procure a
thermometer, Oguebe walked into the living room
dangling the car key and excited about the impending
outing.
"Everybody ready?" he said, expecting excitement and
a unanimous "Yes".
"No, O.G, Baby has a fever!"
"Fever? I thought I just heard her playing around and
babbling with her toys"
"Yes, we just noticed that her brow was very hot and
her body too."

Nena reappeared with two sets of thermometers, one,
rectal and the other, the electronic facial-swipe
version.
She immediately swiped the facial thermometer over
Baby Lydia's brow and as she did so, her countenance
suddenly changed.
"My God! 101.8 degrees!"

As Agesi immediately removing the top dress and the hood that Baby Lydia was already dressed in, Nena swiped the thermometer across her own forehead to compare the readings.

"Mine is 98.6F and that's perfectly normal. And baby's is 101.8" Nena said.

'Yes, even baring the usual slightly higher temperatures for babies, 101.8 is definitely a fever, albeit low grade fever. But it is a fever all the same" Agesi said

Nena was already in a panicky mood. She swiped the thermometer again on Little Baby Lydia's forehead and took the reading.

"102.2 degrees!" She shouted.

She picked up the phone and started dialing Baby Lydia's pediatrician.

"Not so fast, Nena, let's do the very needful first. And remember that baby's doctor is a hundred miles away in Boston. Her documents have not yet been transferred to Sunderland." Oguebe said, breaking his silence but with anxiety written all over his face.

"Yes, dad, but her pediatrician can still advice over the phone." Nena said

"No doubt about that, but let's bring down the temperature first, as much as we can. We can then call her doctor and drive down to the Emergency Room or call the ambulance if need be."

Nena was by this time visibly panicking.

"From 101.8 degrees to 102.2 degrees within so short a time! This is not good. I hope she does not convulse on our hands! And there was no sign of any ear infection, chest infection or urinary tract infection whatsoever." Nena said, her pediatric posting scenarios coming ineffectually to mind.

"Lots of things could be responsible for childhood fever, Nena. Have you thought of the various viral infections which can take you unawares?" Oguebe said.

As father and daughter briefly theorized over possible causes, Agesi was more practical. She had removed the excess clothing on the baby and had procured the pediatric antipyretics which the family had purchased over the counter from a nearby pharmacy chain, a few weeks earlier, "just in case".
At the time of purchase of the acetaminophen infants' oral suspension, neither Agesi nor Nena thought they were going to use it so soon.
The temperature was soon brought down with pediatric antipyretic syrup.
After a wait of four hours, the transient perspiration on the baby's forehead was again replaced by a second spike of the temperature to 103 degrees Fahrenheit.
The plans about dining out were consequently replaced by an unplanned drive to the pediatric wing of the nearby Bay State Medical Center.

Baby Lydia was into her first experience of a childhood fever. It was one that came on very suddenly, one that had sent jitters down the spines of her unprepared mother and grandparents.

Finding a parking space was difficult at the hospital parking lot. It was therefore thought that the clinic was going to be very congested. However, when Nena and her parents got to the reception desk at the pediatric wing of the hospital there was only one patient waiting. Attention to patients was incredibly fast and efficient, and it was such a good thing as it helped shorten the anxiety of parents of sick babies.

Baby Lydia had again started playing following a
repeat dose of antipyretics. But it was obvious that
since the causative agent of the fever had not been
identified and addressed, that the temperature would
rise again as soon as the effect of the antipyretic wore
off.

The baby was promptly registered and examined. As
anticipated, the temperature on examination had
again climbed to 102 degrees Fahrenheit.

Preliminary tests revealed none of the common causes
of childhood fever. A conclusion of viral infection was
arrived at and the baby was placed on temporary
observation while the fever was again brought down
and the baby stabilized and rehydrated.

Luckily for all concerned, getting a vein for the
intravenous infusion did not present a problem for the
pediatric team and Baby Lydia did not cry for too long.
Even though she stopped crying after the first few
minutes of the needle prick, Nena's anxiety was not
assuaged as she continued to stare into the face of
the baby every now and then.

A worried mother, even with her medical background,
would want a miracle to be available if only for her
baby's fever to disappear within a twinkle of an eye.
The fact of being a doctor herself did not appear to
change the undue expectations.

After an observation period of about four hours, the
baby was discharged with medication and necessary
professional advice to the parents.

"It is most likely a viral infection which will clear in the
next seven to ten days." The expert said.

"Ensure you control the temperature with the
prescribed medication. But call back as soon as
possible if the temperature stays up or if further need
arises."

The expert opinion and assurances were like a balm to Nena. The family drove back home with the usually playful and boisterous baby Lydia looking rather quiet even though her fever was considerably down. The smile on her face when Grandma sang to her, her favorite rhythms, was no longer there. It was certain that the fever had weighed her down.

Over the course of the following day the fever was on and off. But the fact of the reassurance from the pediatrician made things easier for the family as the fever-controlling medications were religiously adhered to.
By the evening of the third day the body temperature had fully returned to normal and stabilized.
The loss of appetite and the attendant lethargy however lingered on for a further two days.
By the sixth day the boisterous little lady was once again all smiles.

The few days of fever appeared to have set back the little lady in the development of her milestones. She had almost perfected in walking without support. She had indeed started brisk walking resembling running on carpeted floors. That was before the onset of the fever. After she recovered from the fever however, Baby Lydia was back to her crawling for some three days. She however soon restarted smiling and making repeated efforts to stand and take a few steps forwards.

Yes, to the great joy of Nena, Grandma and Grandpa, Little Baby Lydia was again smiling and insisting on feeding herself. She appeared to have lost weight. Her neck obviously appeared thinner, and apparently longer. And she appeared a little wiser and more suspicious of anything being offered to her from a plastic spoon or from the tip of a hypodermic syringe. Those were the "instruments" which reminded her of the medications which she was compelled to take when she had her first fever.

The joy of having a well and happy baby is not fully appreciated until parents and grandparents go through the rigors of nursing a sick baby, even when the sickness was as transient as that which warranted only a four hour stay in a hospital.
But the joy was back for Nena, Grandma and Grandpa.
And Baby Lydia had once again started to bounce up and down the bed. And she had quickly made up for the lost time in taking many more walking strides before falling back on her thighs.
She obviously was a leaner but wiser and more mature Little Baby Lydia.

Chapter 22

LEARNING THE FIRST WORDS

At nine months Baby Lydia had started babbling. She tried to repeat hand gestures. She also at one year tried to incoherently stick out her hand to mimic "Bye-bye" when a family member or visitor was leaving the house and she was told to say "Bye-bye". Often, she would stick out her hand in the farewell greeting sign which would continue long after the person being addressed had left.

Her attention to people as they spoke became more obvious. She did not disguise her gaze on the lips of any speaker. She would rather focus her gaze piercingly on the lips of whoever was speaking when she was around. If she was being carried up the shoulders when the speaker spoke, she would occasionally attempt to grab the lips of the speaker with her little outstretched fingers.

If there was more than one person in the room, Baby Lydia would sharply turn to the direction of whoever was speaking and focus attention on the person's lips. Thereafter she would try to imitate the speaker with some incomprehensible words. Her words were limited to 'ba, ba, ba" or "taa, taa, taa".

As Baby Lydia spoke, she displayed a set of four brilliantly-white upper and four lower incisor teeth. The eruption of the teeth had slightly changed the shape of the face to a more mature baby's face as different from an infant's face. Nena had gotten baby's ear lobes pierced. And so, with her baby-ear-rings and ribbon-adorned hair, little Baby Lydia had become "an adorable little lady" according to Grandma's description.

Baby Lydia had also become much more active and more participatory in activities around her.
As she watched Grandpa and Grandma wave to her and say "Grandpa" or "Grandma", she would stretch out her hand and incoherently twist her hand randomly in all directions. Within two weeks of "practice" of the art of hand-waving and attempts at twisting her tongue, she would wave back clumsily and say Taaa-Taa or Maaa-maa.
And as she waved she would occasionally try to clumsily repeat monosyllabic words like "ma" and "da".
"Grandpa" and "Grandma" were still too tongue-twisting for little Baby Lydia to pronounce.

The words grandma and grandpa were often demonstrated pointing at the human persons. Baby Lydia would look at the persons demonstrated but would not follow the words. Those words were obviously too complicated for her to follow.
The words "grandma and "grandpa" were nevertheless repeatedly demonstrated.
Baby Julia would often choose words of her own to represent the repeated words. Her most frequently repeated words for grandma and grandpa were the same: "ta-ta".

"Da-da" was the easiest words for her. All other words followed that pattern.

"It is necessary to teach Baby Lydia to pronounce the words "Daddy" along with the words "Ma-ma" or "M-o-omy", Agesi suggested.
"Yes, point at, or demonstrate the physical person in each case. That way, the baby would associate the word with the person in question." Oguebe concurred.

Yes, there was a Ma-ma around to point to. And so, Baby Lydia could readily relate to a physical person in attempting to pronounce that word. But there was no physical person around to point to in teaching her to pronounce the word "daddy" at the stage of formation of that word.
Yes, there was a dad but that was for two weeks and before Baby Lydia was able to recognize the physical person. At the time when a physical dad needed to be pointed to, the latter was some thousands of miles across the oceans. Perhaps circumstances beyond either party's control made it impossible for Daa-daa and Maa-maa and daughter to be together at those crucial stages of their daughter's life. Perhaps it would have been better planned. But whatever be the case, there was adorable Baby Lydia, daily bringing joy and fulfilment to the lives of all who beheld her innocence and her enchanting smile.
It was nevertheless hoped that Baby Lydia would still be able to pronounce and recognize daddy when the latter would be available.
"Thank God, for caring Grandpa and Grandma, on whose shoulders Baby Lydia could cry when offended by mom", Nena usually said whenever Little Baby Lydia chose to be naughty, or when she chose to throw tantrums.

Meanwhile Nena never failed to repeat the word "daddy" each time she said "mommy". That way, she probably felt that Baby Lydia would learn both words simultaneously even if it meant associating the two words with only a single individual at that time, her mom.

Chapter 23

THE LIGHT AT THE END OF THE TUNNEL

Difficulties and unpleasantness tended to make any twenty-four-hour period appear endless.
But the joy of having Baby Lydia around made a full year of baby-sitting appear like mere weeks for Grandma and Grandpa.

Nena had successfully, not only followed up her requirements for graduation, but she had also successfully compensated for all the missed school work and clinicals. She had also completed all outstanding work and was ready for graduation on schedule with the rest of her class mates.
Not only did she complete her schedule in good time she also scored a Grade Point Average of 3.8, one of the ten highest in her graduating class. It was a very big surprise not only to Agesi and Oguebe, but more so to Nena's classmates most of who were indeed very cooperative with Nena in her quest to catch up with missed lectures. One of Nena's close friends Sarah was particularly helpful and had availed Nena of taped recordings of many of the lectures which Nena had missed during the first three weeks that she was off classes immediately following her child-delivery.

It was time again for the yearly commencement exercises when the graduating students would receive their ceremonial certificates in activities that were very much publicized. It was to be the high point of the academic year's activities when parents, family members and friends were invited to celebrate with their loved ones in a public ceremonial award of diplomas.

By the time that the ceremony was holding a number of students might not have actually completed their practical requirements for the award of the diplomas. But as long as they had passed the required Board exams and satisfied the other requirements they would participate in the commencement exercises with the rest of the class. But they would not receive their physical diplomas until they had satisfied all the practical and clinical requirements.

Nena was within the group that had passed the required Board Exams and the written exams but still had some clinical procedures to complete. Yes, even in spite of her having a baby during the course, she had passed all the written and practical exams but she still had a few clinical procedures to complete on some patients. She was confident that as long as her patients turned up, that she would complete the necessary requirements within a few weeks.

The commencement activities were very grand. The graduating students were smartly dressed in their academic gowns.

Baby Lydia too was gorgeously dressed ready to participate alongside her mom. The school authorities were gracious enough to allow babies delivered during the course of the students' courses to participate alongside their mothers and to be carried along on stage with their mothers during the conferment of the Diploma.

Baby Lydia was upbeat throughout the morning of the convocation day. Could she have sensed that it was Mom's big day?

As in-depth as medical science had gone, and as thorough as the study of child psychology had progressed, there appeared still to be no credible study of the inner workings of the minds of little babies.

No, none that was known to Nena and her parents, whereby Baby Lydia's feelings on her mom's graduation day could be fully known.

And so, as she was strapped down on her car seat prior to setting out to the convocation venue Baby Lydia kept babbling and smiling in apparent admiration of the ribbons on her hair and the lovely flowers on her new commencement dress. Her mom's dangling academic cap was also a major attraction for her.

Early at the busy convocation hall, Baby Lydia appeared to be the cynosure of all eyes. She comported herself every inch like a well-groomed little lady.

There were two other babies who also came in baby-strollers to the graduation ceremony.

Baby Lydia was the youngest of the three babies who attended. She looked very radiant in the baby stroller as she "followed" at a distance behind her mom in the baby stroller pushed along by Grandma.

After the many speeches from the Dean and faculty and the recitation of the physician's oath, it was time for presentation of the token certificates and the most anticipated aspect of the day's event: the individual photo-ups for the graduating students with members of faculty.

Nena would not miss the opportunity of carrying Baby Lydia along with her up the podium. It was the high point for both mother and daughter as Baby Lydia was carried up to the podium where she was supposed to pose for the long-awaited epic photo of her mom being handed her Diploma by the Dean of the faculty. The handing over of the diploma was supposed to be photographed by the official professional photographer as well as by whosoever was interested in taking a private snapshot.

Grandpa and Grandma were sitting some distance away in the section of the large hall made for invitees. The events on stage were beamed on large screens for the advantage of the invitees sitting at a distance from the stage.

Nena had proudly come to carry Baby Lydia from Grandma for the photo-up when her name was about to be announced. She was praying in her mind that Baby Lydia who all through the morning had been happy and playful, would continue in her happy mood so that the long-awaited professionally-done Diploma hand-over photo would be very good. She had hoped that both she and Baby Lydia would be smiling broadly as the photo was taken. Each of the three parties, the Dean, the candidate and her baby were expected to be beaming with smiles in the once-in-a-lifetime photo.

But, alas, one of the three parties expected to be smiling broadly in the photo, was deeply asleep! Baby Lydia was in a deep sleep in her baby-stroller when Mom went to carry her up to the podium. Grandma had a short while earlier observed decreased activities from the lady in the stroller. She had tried very hard to keep Baby Lydia awake by dangling toys in front of her. But none of the attempts at keeping the little lady awake had worked. The baby's eyes could easily be seen to be closing repeatedly and her head was gently bending forward even as the toys were being dangled in front of the richly-dressed "graduating lady". Finally, the little lady, resplendent in her richly-embroidered graduation gown fell fully asleep just before Nena came to carry her for the memorable photo with the Dean on the podium!

Obviously worn out by the long preparation as well as by the heavy milk meal that she was given a short while earlier, Baby Lydia was deeply asleep in her mom's arms as both graduating mother and daughter ascended the podium to the cheers of the assembled crowd. Nena's classmates and friends who knew the double ordeal that their friend had gone through cheered the most.
Even with the little princess sleeping soundly in her mother's arms, it was the crowning moment of it all. Neither the cheers nor the loud applause could wake Little Baby Lydia from her slumber.

The little angel was not awake to witness her mom's great moment. Yet the photographers and the video cameramen captured it all for Nena, her friends, her family and indeed for posterity.
And so, even as Nena and the Dean smiled broadly at the photographer, Baby Lydia dozed peacefully in her mother's arms.

Even when Nena slightly agitated her to see if she could wake up to be captured awake in one of the pictures, the big girl slept soundly. If she were a little older, perhaps she might have snored a little. But no, she slept gently and quietly in the arms of her mother even at the latter's moment of glory.

But the somnolence of one of the attendees, did not diminish the magnitude of the success story.
"Baby Lydia chose to sleep rather than disrupt the events", Nena said.
"If she were fully awake the camera might capture her eyes, but she might also be frightened by the large crowd and disrupt the events with loud crying. And so, it is a good thing that she chose to sleep", Nena said.
An elated mother obviously wanted to proffer some excuses for her little baby-daughter.
But everybody understood.
"Yes", Agesi said in support. "Baby Lydia decided to sleep at the right time. If she was yelling or feeling very cranky, the award ceremony might have been greatly disturbed" Agesi told the many inquisitive guests who were stretching their necks to catch a glimpse, not as much of the real graduating student, but more of her sleeping little baby-girl.

As the ceremony ended and the graduating students filed out as ceremoniously as they had entered, a flurry of photo-taking followed in the adjoining reception hall.

Nena had finally graduated with her classmates. She was confident that the few remaining clinical cases which she had outstanding would be completed within two weeks.

Two weeks elapsed like two days and Agesi readily completed the two clinical cases which she had outstanding. Her patients had cooperated very much with her and she got everything done much earlier than she expected.

"The job has been done, and, it was successfully done.
I set out for the course as an individual
And we came home with the certificate as two individuals.
The road had been rough.
But it smoothened out like carpet-grass when it was most needed.
An initial apparent thick cloud of fear had appeared to obstruct the view to success.
But a resolute spirit had been able to successfully surmount the odds.
And the clouds were dispelled as steam from a whistling kettle
And the reward was immense for hard work and dedication
And the doors opened up like sweet petals of an early spring flower.
And the main recipient of the honor, was Little Baby Lydia.
She indeed was an active participant even in a sleeping mode at the graduation venue".
Nena ruminated

"Little Baby Lydia slept throughout the graduation and award ceremony in which she was supposed to be a participant."

Chapter 24

THE FINAL RETURN TO SUNDERLAND

Nena's studies in Boston had been completed
But the lease on her rented apartment in Dorchester
was still in force. She still had one full month
outstanding in the contract. By the terms of the
leasing contract she could not cancel before one full
year. Even when she did not need the apartment any
longer she still had to fulfil the full year of lease
payments.
Rather than break the lease and pay the attendant
penalties, Nena decided to pay the rent for the
remaining one month even while physically living in
Sunderland. Meanwhile she arranged to move her
property into a self-storage until the end of the lease
when she would hand the keys to the apartment back
to the apartment managers.
She loaded her personal effects into the trunk and
inside of her car and drove down to the family home
in Sunderland. She thereafter dropped her car in
Sunderland and returned back to Boston by bus to
finally clear the apartment in company of her parents
and her biggest treasure, Baby Lydia.
It was such a moment of joy and fulfilment as she
bade goodbye to Boston.
Baby Lydia relaxing in her car-seat alongside her mom
at the back seat of the car.

"Three Little Monkeys Jumping on the Bed", Little Baby Lydia's favorite music played from her baby iPad which was strategically positioned at the side of the baby car-seat.

Even as young as she still was, each time that particular song played, Little Baby Lydia would be seen to stop whatever she was doing and remain very attentive. As soon as the music stopped she would be seen to restart kicking or flapping of her hands.

But the music was partially drowned by the louder stereo music from the CD of the car. Perhaps Baby Lydia could still hear her favorite music even amidst the sound of the adult music. Perhaps the mixed music from the two instruments constituted another form of music for Little Baby Lydia.

The mixed music could well have been music different from what the adults were listening to.

"It had been a most successful adventure to Boston." Nena said.

"Yes indeed" Agesi said. "We first came from Sunderland to Boston as three: your dad, your mom and you. Now we will go back to Sunderland as four: grandpa, grandma, doctor-mom, and a fourth member, Little Baby Lydia. It is all to God's glory!" Agesi solemnly said as Nena finally shut the outer door of the Boston rented apartment.

The family was finally on their way back to their family home in Sunderland. With Oguebe on the driver's seat the family cruised happily under Boston's many bridges into the 90-West Massachusetts Turnpike away from the great City of Boston.

Unlike in most other trips to, or from Boston, Baby Lydia scarcely slept. She appeared to know that she was going to have her mom with her for a longer time than at any other time so far since her eleven months of birth. She kept gazing at Nena with her head almost steadily turned to the right side in the direction of her mom. She babbled and smiled broadly at every jerk of the car and at every turn.

For Little Baby Lydia it certainly promised to be a wonderful re-union with Mom after only two months of continuous living together prior to her movement to Sunderland to live with Grandma and Grandpa.

If one-year-old babies could talk well, Baby Lydia would perhaps narrate to Mom how much she missed her. She would have narrated how she missed the warm feeling of breastfeeding of those first two to three weeks before she started on pumped breastmilk and bottle feeding on baby-formula.

"I will probably like to get back to breast milk, now that Mom is through with her studies," she appeared to say.

But unfortunately, that was not to be, any longer. The breast milk had gone dry. But mother's love and affection still flowed in abundance and waxed stronger by the day.

Perhaps Little Baby Lydia was aware of the fact that Mom was coming home for good.

Perhaps that was why she was smiling from ear to ear.

Perhaps that was why she was not sleeping in the car seat as she was wont to do during most other travels.

Perhaps she wanted to savor every moment of those initial three hours of the momentarily-interrupted drive from Boston to Sunderland.

Perhaps it was no longer another of the occasional trips by Mom who would head back to Boston first thing the following morning.
Yes, perhaps she was not sure whether Mom would be heading back to Boston the following morning.
But, No! Mom was back to Sunderland for good.
Yes, Mom would remain with her little bundle of joy for many days on end.
She would indeed remain with her little idol non-stop for weeks or months.
She would no longer be a Student-mom.
She would henceforth be a daily Mom for her adorable Little Baby Lydia.

Issues concerning professional practice and Residency for Nena were momentarily placed in the back burner. She had applied for and attended a series of interviews. The matching for Residency Program was still many months away.
But Nena first wanted to have a few weeks of rest before thinking of any, and all offers of jobs. Her most treasured possession Baby Lydia, was the thing uppermost in her mind. She did not want any discussions or anxiety about Residency matching or otherwise to diminish the monumental joy that she had at hand.
And the source of the monumental joy was right there beside her in the baby-cot at the back seat of the car.
The source of the monumental joy was no other than Little Baby Lydia.

The journey back to Sunderland was not stressful in the least. Perhaps the joy of a mission-accomplished lightened the stress. Even Grandpa's occasional craze for plaza pizza or the pressure on him to stop for use of the rest rooms at alternate plazas along the I-90 West Freeway between Boston and Springfield Massachusetts vanished momentarily on that last of the routine trips to, or from Boston. It was not until the family got to Ludlow Plaza some one and a half hours away from Boston, did Oguebe decide to pull into the plaza. That single stop was indeed not out of any pressure but out of sheer fulfilment of an old habit.

The happy family stepped out at Ludlow Plaza to have some snacks.
"I feel as if a large load has been lifted off me", Nena said.
"And me, too" Agesi said.
"And me, the most" Oguebe said.
Oguebe's assertion was certainly not out of a desire to merely toe the line of the discussion.
No, it was a manifestation of genuine relief after many months of apparent reclusion and self-imposed new occupation as a baby-sitter.

And just at that point, Baby Lydia babbled loudly looking from the direction of her mom.
And by a strenuous backwards twisting of her head, she also was able to gaze in the direction of Grandma.
Could she also have been expressing that an equally large load had been lifted off her?
No, it could not have been any large load lifted off her. It could only be some tons of joy, loaded upon Little Baby Lydia!

At least Mom had made her proud by her excellent academic performance even in spite of the extra work-load of looking after her.

For Nena, it was a large load of academic and clinical requirements lifted off her, at least momentarily.
For Agesi, it was the large load of nightly sleeping with one eye open. Grandma hitherto had to take charge of Baby Lydia since after the latter's relocation to Sunderland, from the moment she returned from work every evening; and through the night till the following morning. It was the extra load of daily giving Baby Lydia a much-needed bath every evening and seeing to her feeding intermittently through the night.

And for Grandpa who had borne the brunt of day-care for Baby Lydia for one and a half months in Boston and for many more months in Sunderland, it was a bag of mixed blessings.
The latter would have time to start rebuilding his small business which was as good as being in limbo over the course of his baby-sitting. But at the same time, Grandpa would miss the many-hours-a-day joy of Baby Lydia's boisterous smiles and her recent adventures of crawling under small crevices and tables in the living room and the dining room. He would miss the ungainly-gait walk of the little lady who had recently learnt to walk and even run with outstretched hands. He would soon forget the painstakingly-learnt art of diaper-changing, bottle feeding and rocking a baby to sleep. For many months these had formed part of his daily routine. If there was a professorship in a discipline termed "The Art of Grandpa as a Baby-sitter", perhaps Oguebe would have qualified for the conferment of such a title. Until that was available, Oguebe was content with merely tending to his granddaughter and taking down his daily notes.

"The Art of Grandpa as a Baby-sitter" will be almost an entirely new discipline, perhaps borrowing bits and pieces from the field of Child Psychology and greatly enriching the field of Geriatrics and almost certainly aiding studies of the secrets of longevity and exquisite joy in the elderly.

For, until one experiences the immense happiness of spending a full day watching the faltering first steps and listening to the babbling sounds of one's grandchildren and feeding them with small crumbs of their choice, one would not have truly experienced indescribable joy.

Little Baby Lydia provided full measure of the joys of grandparenting to Oguebe and Agesi.

And to Nena, the little bundle of joy was fulfillment par excellence.

There are certainly millions of Little Baby Lydias out there if only grandpas and grandmas could make out the time. And, of course it can only be possible if the many Nenas that abound, muster the courage to combine intensive academic pursuits with child-rearing.

And, the millions of Oguebes, Agesis and Nenas that abound, each narrating their experiences will greatly enrich our world.

"" I am learning how to cook by peeping
through the gate".

Chapter 25

FINALLY, WITH MOM

As the car took a turn into the drive way of the family home in Sunderland Little Baby Lydia immediately seemed to recognize the familiar surroundings. She uttered some chuckling sounds of joy, displaying her erupting four upper and four lower incisor teeth.
It appeared to be a different Baby Lydia that came back to Sunderland.
The presence of her mom appeared to have added tremendous vitality and boisterousness to Little Baby Lydia.
As soon as she was unstrapped from the baby car-seat, Baby Lydia spread out her arms into the welcoming arms of her mom. The latter had exited the car and had walked over to the baby's side of the car. Smiling Baby Lydia appeared to be saying "finally home with Mom!".

She giggled and as she was lifted out of the car seat, she beat mom gently at the back of the shoulders with her small outstretched palms. She kicked her feet, not out of tantrum or revolt as she sometimes did. No, she was dancing with joy in the arms of her mom. It was a most surprising scenario for Grandpa and Grandma who had rarely seen their little granddaughter so happy or so elated so soon after a long journey.

"Who said that little babies are not very intelligent?" Agesi said.
"Who taught Baby Lydia how to express abundant joy, such as this?" Agesi added.

Grandma stretched out her hands as if making to carry Baby Lydia.
Alas, the little lady had found new love in her mom and had immediately begun to reject her old friends.
She briskly turned away from Grandma and clung tightly to the shoulders of her mom, hiding her face in Mom's chest.
"Are you rejecting me so soon, Baby Lydia?" Grandma asked in feigned disappointment.
Still with outstretched arms, Granma again invited Baby Lydia.
"Come on, baby, Grandma loves you!"
It was then that Baby Lydia appeared to change her mind and turned her face and her outstretched arms towards an appreciative Grandma.
She then uttered her characteristic response at the statement: "Grandma loves you, OK"
"Ka!" she immediately replied in her characteristic manner.
It was a response which she always gave to that statement.
Nobody in the family knew for sure the real meaning of that monosyllabic word "Ka".
Only Baby Lydia knew and understood what it exactly meant.
Perhaps it was an affirmation of the word "OK".
And the little lady never failed to respond with that stereotyped word.
But this time however she deviated from the direction at which she looked each time she responded with that word.

She was not looking at Grandma who told her that she loved her.
No, she was looking at Mom who was now carrying her, and who she knew would henceforth love her much more.

Few things in life could give more joy to parents than seeing their children succeed in things that they have devoted energy and time to.
And fewer things in life can compare with the joy of a grandparent when he or she lifts up a smiling grandchild and holds the latter to his or her bosom.
Such were the blessings which Grandpa Oguebe and Grandma Agesi experienced with Nena and Little Baby Lydia as mother and daughter finally reunited in the family home.
It was a memorable welcome back to Sunderland.

Soon after learning to take the first few steps, running and falling became the order of the day for Little Baby Lydia.
The hands and legs would be spread widely apart as she staggered into each run.
And any obstacle on the way would readily precipitate a fall.
And the little lady enjoyed every step forward that she took.
And the broad smiles on her face were ready evidence of the sense of fulfilment that Little Baby Lydia felt at her learning to walk.

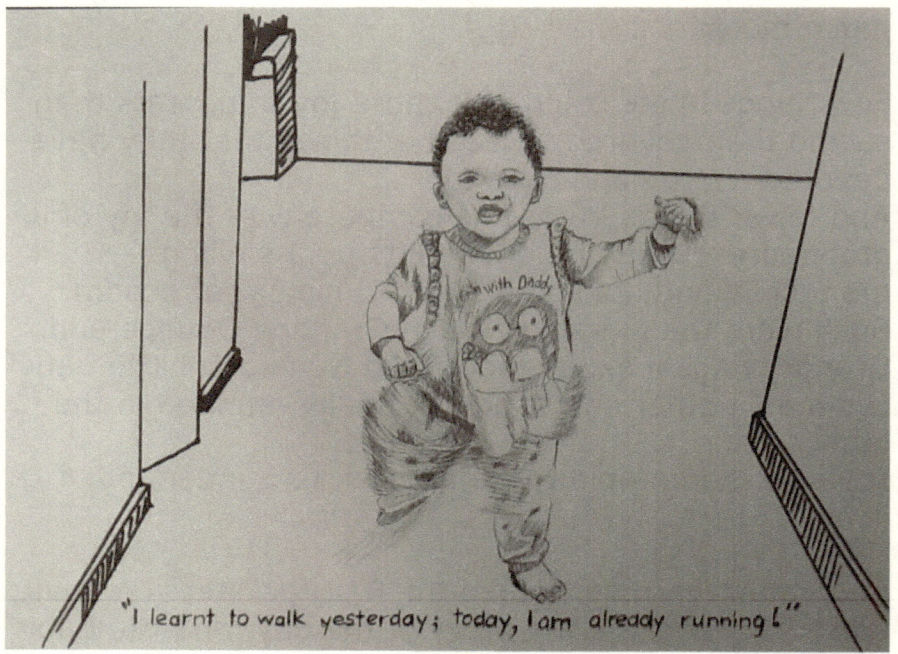

"I learnt to walk yesterday; today, I am already running!"

Chapter 26

THE GRANDPARENTS' TESTIMONY:
"YES, WE MADE IT!"

"Yes, we made it!
All of us did.
All, including any and all who exercise enough
patience to read this testimony.
Nena was the arrowhead.
Agesi and Oguebe were the tools.
But the silent motivator of the challenge was the one
that did not utter a word.
She was the one who even in silence or unintelligible
words dictated the direction as well as the pace.
She was the least in body size, least in age, least in
proffering solutions to problems
But she was the greatest as a source of joy.
And so, it was she who made it the most.
And her name was Baby Lydia
The appendage of "Little", was only a habit and a
misnomer.
For, she was the greatest achiever.
She possessed neither physical coercive powers nor
the powers of words.
But she made things go her way by merely crying or
showing displeasure.
And when she smiled it was automatic stamp of
approval.
She cried when she was hungry or wet.

She also cried when she wanted to sleep.
At other times she cried for inexplicable reasons.
And when she was about six months old she would cry
if she wanted a toy and could not reach it.

And as she approached one year old, she would cry
when she wanted to be carried.
She also cried when her favorite children's rhythm
that was playing suddenly got interrupted.
Again, she made only unintelligible statements at one
year.
Nobody understood her and none could decipher her
babbling.
Yet she was the motivator of the entire challenge.
She was the one around whom almost our entire lives
were fixated for the preceding one year and longer.
She merely reacted to the mention of her name up to
one year.
Nobody her age would be expected fully to answer.
But she turned her head in the direction of the caller,
at the mention of her name.

She did not walk at one year.
But she was faster on her knees than many that ran.
Then she stood and would take a few steps forward.
Thereafter, she would realize that crawling was faster.
And down on her knees she would again go.

And she brought joy and excitement to the family and
all that came across her.
And she continued to do so at every turn.
She did not point to what she wanted at one year.
But at eighteen months she always did.
She would bounce up and down at the sight of her
desired food at one year
And she would sense that chicken was around; it was
her favorite meal.

The smell of cooking chicken always seemed to stir
her appetite.
How she always recognized that her food was around
surprised everyone.
And a sharp cry would ensue if the expected food was
put away.
So sharp were her vision and her sense of smell!

And even as a baby she ruled the house.
And her name was on every lip.
All day long she was the apple of all eyes.
And her name, Baby Lydia.

"Yes, even if it appears as blowing of one's own
trumpets, let it be."
So, says the lizard that survives a fall from a height
and out-runs its pursuers on the ground.

If none congratulates the smart lizard it must
congratulate itself.
When none is there to hail your success, you must hail
yourself.
You must, but with humility, beat your chest.
That way you muster the strength and enthusiasm to
achieve even more.
That way you motivate friends and family to emulate
and to win.
Even while modest, we must also endeavor to
celebrate.
Success celebrated, can only engender more success.
Failure is never an option while dealing with baby-
sitting,
No, not when bountiful source of joy continues to flow
from Little Baby Lydia.

Self-congratulation is no pride
If it is seen by any to be, let it be.

As long as it does not get on the way of others, let it be.
And if it will propel the doer of deeds to do more, let it be.
It can only be a motivator for other grandpas and grandmas, and so, let it be.

Thus, indolence will be given a back seat in all that we do.
And industry and resourcefulness will assume the front burner, so, let it be.
It is only the doers of deeds that propel our world.
Excessive modesty and trepidation hardly ever win the day.

Nothing gets done unless it is done by somebody.
And the doers of great deeds deserve acclamation.
And Baby Lydia and her hardworking mom deserve acclamation
If none acclaims them, they must acclaim themselves.
Thus, the zeal to do more will rule our world.

And industry and courage will be richly rewarded.
Thus, our world will be a better place for all.
Often, to achieve our goals we must also humble ourselves.

What one is, or what one thinks he or she is, has little place in achieving the things that matter.
Humility in little things of life, and sometimes letting go, are where success and happiness begin.
Too much planning or too much care for what will be said are the beginnings of failure.
Spontaneity in the little things of life are the lifelines to success and happiness.
And when family is involved, all ego and husbandry must assume the back seat.

It is best to first do what is necessary before considering what is convenient.
Other considerations must submit to what is of utmost importance in the family.
What society expects, should be of secondary importance to family harmony and cohesiveness.

The decision to subsume any and all ego, convenience and all income to babysit Little Baby Lydia was a worthwhile venture.
And the abiding bonding between grandparents and granddaughter is a jewel of inestimable value.
It was a single arrow that successfully shot two games.

In pursuit of a worthwhile goal some toes of trepidation might be stepped upon.
Some personal gains and things that we treasured the most might be compromised.
And the company of friends might be missed at social events.
But all eyes must at all times remain on the ball.
After success must have been achieved, any necessary amends could be made.
Others failing to play their expected parts must never dampen our enthusiasm.
Alexander Pope had indeed said it all:
"Act well your part, there, all the honor lies".

Any toes that might have been stepped on, with time could be redressed.
And any company and social events that might have been missed will also be assuaged.
It is never too late to make amends after the needful must have been done.
It might be too late to do the needful neglected in the quest for social correctness or what was expected.

As long as the law and the rights of others were not trampled upon in pursuit of industry and success, always do the needful.

"What will I do to make family closer, country greater, and the world a better place?" should always come first.

"What will I do to meet the expectations of my social circles?" should come a distant second.

But the number one achievement and the principal solace remain the double success.

Considerations for Little Baby Lydia's well-being inevitably came first.

The professional certificate and the attendant remunerations came a close second.

Both attained with a single arrow was all-fulfilling indeed.

We had to be babysitters for our daughter to graduate.

And we witnessed the good results that emanated from our resolve.

Baby Lydia was such a joy to behold and we relished the result.

She is worth any and all sacrifices that baby-sitting might have entailed.

And we relish and share the joy emanating from our resolve.

We obviously lost a lot in the eyes of a materialistic society.

But what was gained by investing in a human being is certainly unquantifiable.

The role reversal was not the norm for the society of our birth.

Grandpa as baby-sitter might be unheard of, but we made it happen.

If we did not take the bull by the horns, our granddaughter would have suffered.

And her mother might have missed a once in a life time opportunity to excel.

It was rather absurd in some circles, even in the society that we embraced.

It was not economical and would have been cheaper and more comfortable to contract out the care.

But the bonding and family affection that we imparted can never be quantified.

It looked impossible if not naïve to adopt the path that we treaded.

But the worthy example thus set and the greatness of the warmth and bonding thus built will abide with us for life.

To all Grandmas and Grandpas out there, we share a simple testimony.

And to all daughters and student moms to be, here is our message:

Where there are dads and moms who can spare the time for you, make use of the opportunity.

Get a shot at childbearing if you so desire,

If thirty and above, even if in college, give it a shot.

Even if your spouse or baby's father is nowhere near to help with the care, do the best that you can.

Fulfil your maternity desires while you safely and simply, can.

Careful planning no doubt, is essential for the good of baby and mother.

But the desire for parenthood must not be sheepishly subservient to academic ego and personal comfort.

Motherhood does not come easy at any stage and may be fraught with challenges.

But it is richly rewarding when all is done, and it will be relished in the end.

Where there is a will in life, though tortuous, there will always be a way.

Dispel any and all fears or trepidation where these strongly supervene.
The rewards are immense, much more than many can readily imagine.
The mud-smeared fingers in the pond of unpleasantness, at the end, ensure the oily lips.
Making and raising a baby even as a student has its peculiar joys and sense of fulfilment.
The initial challenges are certainly there; but where in life are there no challenges?
There do not have to be a grandma or a grandpa to help out with the care.
Other viable forms of care invariably exist.
There is no perfect time for raising a family because different challenges, in each situation invariably arise.
Every stage in life has its peculiar challenges.
Procrastination they say is the thief of time.
And the worst thing that any can fear, is fear itself.

A childless youthful life may serve its purposes.
But where will humanity be heading towards if the majority opt for a childless family situation?
A lonely old age is never envisioned while we are young.
Until it becomes too late it is not often realized.
In the enticing joy of youth, it is easy not to look beyond the present.
A Baby Lydia curtailed our present freedoms; sure it did, but what does it matter at the end of the day?
Our tomorrow will surely be brighter with a Little Baby Lydia present, to bring the cheer.
A lonely senior home may be awaiting the childless as well as the forgotten mom,
Even when sacrifices are forgotten, the pictures that memorialize the childhoods will at least be our solace.
Where there are no memories at all, the solitude is more resounding.

And where today's convenience supersedes tomorrow's companionship, a bleak and lonely future is assured.

Machines, social media networking and rented companionship can do quite a bit for aging humanity.
Yes, the scopes in "modern living" and "senior living" enlarge by the day.
But nothing can substitute for family, no matter the extent of rented care.
Even when younger family choose to forget, we can hold the photos to our chests.
Those images of many Baby Lydias can never be erased or substituted.
In the end, it is the human mind alone that is embosomed with the love that truly matters.

Two walking as one and one working as two can surmount all challenges.
There exists a Mommy, a Nena, and a Baby Lydia in most, that may so desire.
Again, there is little to fear in starting a family as a student, except fear itself.
The worst that can happen is an extension of time.
But where does the rush in life really lead if one may ask?
The mere understanding that one is working not just for self but also for an unborn baby invariably makes for added zeal.
Perhaps the natural hormones that come on with pregnancy will help combat any attendant stresses.
And as the baby arrives and the academic honors come on, the double blessings are savored.
There is a Nena in every mommy and a Baby Lydia always to make one's day.

And when two walk up the podium to receive one Diploma, it's like doubling the Diploma without extra cost.
And the sense of fulfilment is such that it endures a life time at no added expense.

"Yes, we made it, to the glory of God.
All of us jointly made it, including the reader.
Parents, grandparents, family, friends and well-wishers, all, to some extent played their parts.
And Nena made it to graduation in spite of any and all odds.
The weariness after the day's work obviously did pose challenges.
And the anxiety over the approaching nightfall obviously took its toll.
Yet the cheer on the faces of all participants always remained unmistakable.
And the determination to succeed and make a difference certainly prodded us on.

An eye on the ball was well maintained and we never relented in our commitment
Even when a baby's father became nowhere near to assist, the pain of the vacuum was borne with equanimity.
Avoidable or unavoidable absence of a parent at a moment of greatest need should not be seen as the end of the world.
Such a situation for whatever reasons, should make friends and family to step up to the challenge.
Family and friends invariably stepped up to the challenge and Little Baby Lydia cheered everyone up with her adorable smiles.
There will always be help on the way for all who muster the courage to persevere.

A month or two of paternity care, no doubt can take its toll on some young and inexperienced father.
Lack of experience might also lead to poor planning and regrettable decisions.
But all is well that ends well, as the old saying goes.
Any trading of blames for lack of preparedness or wrong decisions can only be counterproductive.
The important thing in all difficult situations is for a solution to any challenges to be found.
All that must be ensured was that the baby and her parents must in the end do well.
Any attendant hardships or regrets are irrelevant but can provide useful lessons for other young people as they plan their lives.

The attendant joys are many, and they must be celebrated with gratitude to God and a caring society.
Good judgment and hard work will always remain the bedrock of success even in family decisions.
The shenanigans of man must take a back seat for all that we should care.
The sun will still rise from the East and set in the West and the future is bound to be bright.
For all those who plan well and endure the necessary sacrifices associated with hard work and perseverance there can be nothing but smiles in the end.
And provided we persevere, all stresses and initial fears will be mere stories for the future.
Positive thinking and a determination to succeed will invariably lead to attainment of the desired results.
The latter worked for Nena and Little Baby Lydia and they will inevitably work for all else.

Yes, the grandparents had to reassume a near-forgotten role.
And Nena had to attend antenatal clinics while her classmates rehearsed and practiced.

And she had to sit up for hours each day pumping breast milk to store for a newborn that would have required her presence.
And she had to defer some class tests if they conflicted with her doctor's appointment days.
But she equally was aware of the need to care for another life.
Baby Lydia was too young to express her joys at the success of a well-executed plan.
Yet, the tell-tale signs of happiness were virtually written all over her face.
As she readily smiled to Mom, Grandma and Grandpa the joy was complete.
These were regular faces that she had seen from birth, and certainly, she will never forget.

Yes, the innocent little baby must have, and did have, all the needed love.
And any additional needed care must never be denied.
The joy that Baby Lydia brought, far surpassed any and all stresses and sacrifices.

What greater joy could grandparents have than playing and smiling with a strong and happy grandchild?
The little bundle of joy would climb around and all over Grandpa and Grandma.
Even as Grandpa sat watching television the little angel would scratch at his wrinkled fingers.
And she would grab and spread out the fingers and stare at the nails.
And her own finger nails were as sharp as razor if unattended to, for a week or two.
And Grandpa's withered face would receive some cuts from Little Baby Lydia's nails.
And Grandma would thus be reminded that there was some work to do.

Little Baby Lydia's nails needed to be cut, at least to spare her own, and Grandpa's faces.

Though the hands trembled and the knees hurt
And though the tongue questioned why a near-forgotten role should be re-played
Yet, the tiny little hand that grasped a grandparent's thumb conferred all the joys.
And if she beamed a smile on Grandma or Grandpa, the latter's' joys were complete.
The heart was filled with love for all we cared.
No matter the excuses, the needful in care was always rendered.
God's gift in a Baby Lydia was worth more than any could imagine.

Again, there is a Baby Lydia in every Nena out there.
And even where there was no Grandma or Grandpa, there will invariably be a close relative or a friend who cares.
And social welfare would be a source of assistance of last resort.
And the Commonwealth of Massachusetts and indeed most states are known to be great and efficient in care for any who may be distressed.
What is required most, is the resolve to plan well and take the initial first steps, however faltering they may appear.

For Baby Lydia and her parents, it looked as if an old familiar story was about to play out.
It might not be a full replay but it tended to look like one.
It was one that was told relating to a one-time player in the highest level of governance in the land.
It was the story of a most-notable family that American history will never forget

It was a memorable tale of a Grandpa and a Grandma stepping up to the challenges of an absentee father.
Family love inevitably triumphed and overcomes any, and all similar challenges.
And, courtesy of God's Own Country, the subject ended up as the world's number one.
Little Baby Lydia even when she does not become President
As sure as the day follows the night, she stands qualified.
And she will make a positive difference in more ways than one.
The glass ceilings have been shattered or are about to be shattered
And she is imbibing the same humaneness, and the same family love from all around her.
Mom, Grandpa, Grandma, uncles and aunts have all showered their love on her.
And, even from the very early days of her life she is being brought up to be humane.

Yes, Grandma and Grandpa had, for a while, to relearn some forgotten roles.
It has been a story that would all inspire.
History is replete with replays of initially sad or naughty stories that turned sweet at the end.
They are stories which might appear cumbersome but which never clogged the history books.
They are stories which urge us never to surrender or see any situation as sad or insurmountable.
But whether sweet or sad, humanity always learns and is always richer with every story.
And, the sweet stories got sweeter by being retold.
And, even the sad stories got sweetened when retold with love and understanding.
They got sweetened by the knowledge and lessons which they conferred on man.

And "Little Baby Lydia" as the story, is one that greatly motivates.
It is one that greatly enriches our humanity and our world.

EPILOGUE

SOME NIGHTS OF WAKEFULNESS,
SOME NIGHTS OF JOY

Some nights might have been long by the standards
of man.
Most Grandma and Grandpa would wish to have quiet
and restful nights.
Most had played their parts when it was their turns.
Most had in their child-rearing ages, faced the
stresses of wakeful nights.
A few would wish not to be awakened by a baby
crying for bottle-feeding or diaper change.
Every little baby has his or her peculiar situations
And so, it was, with Little Baby Lydia.

Her repeated turning and shrill cry was no burden to
any weary Grandma or Grandpa.
No, the sound was pleasant and it brought spicy
variety by breaking the monotonous silence of the
night.
And it was good it did.
Too much monotony, too much silence that aging and
retirement confer, could indeed be a bore to some
senior's bones.

There was never a sigh from Grandma or Grandpa on
being awakened by the cry.
We knew at all such occasions that our little bundle of
joy needed our attention.
And we rendered the same with every loving care.

And the eventual gentle smile did all the soothing, and
compensated for any sleep that we might have
missed.

The fragile little human was our joy to behold.
We witnessed a new life come into the world.
We heard the first shrill cry that gladdened the heart.
And we witnessed the index finger that pointed in our direction as if to signal greatness.
And we beheld the brilliant deep-brown eyes that appeared to acknowledge us all.
And we knew that we had a notable role to play.
And any needed guidance or care must never be denied.
As any little stress must be totally borne with the deepest love.

And we were hardly ever disappointed or burdened by our little bundle of joy.
We were invariably handsomely compensated by an initial toothless smile.
And when eventually the teeth erupted they were beautiful and brilliantly-white.
And they erupted at the same time as those little conversations from our little angel.
And the conversations sometimes were initiated in a baby language which we could not understand.
And the conversation would be initiated after a full meal of milk.
And they came on in babbles, and often when everyone else was expected to be asleep.
Yes, they were initiated sometimes after midnight in a language which no one really understood.
But even when we did not understand Baby Lydia's babbling language we still greatly treasured the attempt to communicate.
And we were invariably handsomely compensated by early morning enchanting smiles.
Those were not any falsely-enchanting smiles of some distant TV entertainers.

They were not any feigned smiles that might emanate from some unpredictable maiden.
Or any deceitful smiles that might only be as sincere as the mere parting of lips.
No, they were true-life enchanting smile from some little angel who was not capable of pretense.
They were very genuine and deep-seated smiles of love and appreciation.
They were smiles from a lovely granddaughter, Little Baby Lydia.